'I'd like to have
The only thing i

Chloe took a deep
moment she was going to tell him. But only
so much. Not the real truth.

'It will have to be a quick drink because I
want to get home to my children.'

Complete disbelief figured on Demetrius's
face. 'Children? You have children? But you
said you were only married for six months.'

'Long enough for me to have twins,' she said
defensively.

'Twins. I'm amazed!' Suddenly Demetrius
seemed to recover his composure. 'What are
they? Girls? Boys? How old are they?'

'Two girls, age seven…well, nearly eight.'

She desperately tried to hide her anxiety as
she saw Demetrius's shocked expression
change. Why had she admitted they were
nearly eight?

Dear Reader

I've been in love with the Greek islands for many years, especially the island of Ceres (not its real name). It's so relaxing you want to stay there for ever, wandering in the hills along deserted paths before going down to one of the spectacularly beautiful bays where you can swim in the crystal-clear waters of the Mediterranean.

While lazing on a beach in the hot sun one day—as you do!—I started to get the idea for a story about three sisters, the daughters of a famous surgeon, all of them medically qualified, who go out to live on Ceres and work in the hospital. There would be a wonderful sense of community in the hospital, just as there is among the delightful, friendly people on this idyllic island. So I started writing…

Greek Island Hospital was born. DR DEMETRIUS'S DILEMMA is the second book in the trilogy and follows the story of Sara's sister Chloe and the gorgeous Dr Demetrius. Look out for the story of Sara and Chloe's sister Francesca—the enigmatic doctor—later in the year.

I hope you'll enjoy reading these stories as much as I've enjoyed writing them. Being on the island of Ceres with Sara, Chloe and Francesca has given me hours of pleasure. I hope you'll feel the same when you put the final book down.

Happy reading

Margaret Barker

DR DEMETRIUS'S DILEMMA

BY

MARGARET BARKER

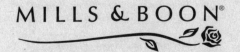

MILLS & BOON®

All the characters in this book have no existence outside the imagination of the author, and have no relation whatsoever to anyone bearing the same name or names. They are not even distantly inspired by any individual known or unknown to the author, and all the incidents are pure invention.

*First published in Great Britain 2003
Harlequin Mills & Boon Limited,
Eton House, 18-24 Paradise Road, Richmond, Surrey TW9 1SR*

© Margaret Barker 2003

ISBN 0 263 83445 X

*Set in Times Roman 10½ on 12 pt.
03-0503-49866*

*Printed and bound in Spain
by Litografia Rosés, S.A., Barcelona*

CHAPTER ONE

CHLOE continued to wave goodbye to Rachel and Samantha, who were still jumping up and down excitedly on the shore. When the boat rounded the corner of Nimborio Bay and sailed towards Ceres harbour, she lost sight of her beautiful little daughters. Chloe always felt a certain sense of sadness as she headed off for hospital, leaving the twins behind. She would have loved to have spent more time with them this morning, but she needed to be at the hospital early today.

Some mornings there was time to play on the shore, skimming stones across the bay. Other mornings they would go out into the garden at the back of the house, through the little gate and climb up the steep path on the hillside where they would gather sweet-smelling herbs or simply sit in the sunshine, enjoying the fabulous scenery.

But not today! At least she knew her children were well cared for and happy when she wasn't with them. Chloe's mother, Pam, had been more like a second mother than a grandmother to the twins ever since Chloe had gone back to nursing. Pam adored her grandchildren and out here on Ceres, helped by the capable Maria, she enjoyed being in charge of them while Chloe was working at the hospital. Later this morning, Pam or Anthony, Chloe's father, or sometimes both of them, would drive the children to Ceres school.

The twins loved going to school and meeting their Greek and English friends, and when they got home this evening Chloe would make sure she spent as much time as possible with her precious daughters.

She gazed out across the water, away from Ceres town to the wide stretch of the Mediterranean, clear and sparkling in the morning sunlight, remembering for a brief moment that holiday she'd spent here before the twins were born. The joy of sailing out there on the water without a care in the world.

She gave herself a mental shake. It wasn't often she allowed herself to daydream. That was one of the useless self-indulgent activities she'd discarded long ago. It was totally unproductive to dwell on what might have been if only…

She shivered, feeling as if someone had suddenly walked across her grave. Why on earth she should suddenly start thinking about that brief time in her former life she simply couldn't imagine. She was experiencing a weird feeling now, rather like a premonition of impending danger…

'You OK, Chloe?'

Manolis, the ever helpful boatman, handyman, gardener, married to their incomparable domestic help Maria, paused, holding the mooring rope in one hand as he looked enquiringly at Chloe.

'I'm fine, Manolis,' she said, affecting a false brightness in her tone of voice.

Manolis wasn't taken in by her answer but he turned away to get on with mooring the boat.

'Well, that's OK, then. You looked a bit peaky just now. Wouldn't want them to have to close the hospital today because their most important sister is ill.'

Chloe laughed. 'I'm not that important!'

Manolis threw the rope towards a mooring post and leapt ashore. 'That's not what I've heard,' he said, tying the rope securely round the post. 'Maria told me you're in charge of the whole of one floor in the hospital. Very important, she said you were. The hospital would grind to a halt if you didn't work there.'

He held out his hand towards Chloe. She grasped it and stepped onto the quayside.

'Well, yes, it's a responsible job,' Chloe conceded. 'But I'm simply part of an excellent team. Lots of skilled medical staff.'

'Same time tonight, Chloe?' Manolis asked, getting back in the boat.

'I'll have to phone you during the day, Manolis. I'm not sure what time I can get off duty. We've got a new doctor who specialises in obstetrics coming today and Dr Michaelis, our medical director, has asked me to spend some extra time with him to show him the ropes.'

'Haven't seen Dr Michaelis for a while.' Manolis looked thoughtful. 'Everything OK between him and Sara?'

Chloe smiled. 'Fabulous, according to Sara. She and Michaelis rush home to their love nest whenever they're both off duty. They're planning their wedding this summer. Probably August.'

'We're already in June, so not long now. Hope I'll be invited!' Manolis grinned as he turned away to start the engine.

'Of course you will, Manolis,' Chloe called above the noise of the engine.

As she moved across the uneven cobblestones of the quayside, stepping round a couple of boxes of freshly caught fish, Chloe was thinking about the romance between her sister Sara and Michaelis. It had been a whirlwind affair which had seemed doomed to failure for a while. But in the end they'd realised they were made for each other. Love had certainly conquered all!

She stifled the sigh that rose to her lips. She was so happy for Sara but it was no use getting all gooey-eyed when she had to start thinking about the day's work ahead of her. Yes, it was going to be a busy day, but she loved her work. Work was the panacea which had helped her to forget the crises in her life.

Would she have done things differently if she could put the clock back? Chloe slowed her step as she walked up the steep slope that led to the hospital. It was futile to conjecture what she should have done. And anyway, why was she suddenly becoming so introspective? What was done was done. As her grandmother used to say, she'd made her bed and now she must lie in it. It was all in the past and she couldn't go back. She could only go forward—and she'd better get a move on if she was going to get through her busy schedule today.

Walking in through the main door of the hospital, she found herself immediately called over to the reception desk.

'Chloe!' Michelle, the young Australian receptionist, called to her. 'Dr Michaelis has asked if you'll go to his office as soon as you get in. He's arrived! The new doctor.' Michelle lowered her voice. 'Very handsome! You'll like him.'

Chloe gave her a wry smile. 'As long as he can do his job, I don't care what he looks like, Michelle.'

She turned away quickly and made for the female staff cloakroom. It was true. She had absolutely no interest in what the new man looked like. She'd learned from bitter experience to take no personal interest in the opposite sex. Romance and everything that went with it weren't for her any more. Anyway, this handsome new doctor was probably married—as she was to her work.

Moving aside a large cardboard box of toilet paper and

some piles of soap, she made for the mirror to do something about the disastrous mess of her long blonde hair. Coming across in the boat was a wonderful way of getting to work in the morning, but the sea breeze always played havoc with her hair.

Stepping out of her cotton skirt and blouse, she pulled on her navy blue uniform, clasping the silver buckle at her waist. Thank heavens for the air-conditioning! It was going to be hot outside today but at least the hospital was kept at an even, workable temperature.

Looking at herself in the mirror, she raked a comb through the tangles. Her hair fell smoothly back into place again, reaching down to her shoulders. Swiftly, she pulled it back into a tight knot, before fixing the tiny white cap in place.

As she made her way out again, she glanced around at the piles of supplies around her. There must be somewhere all these items could be stored, apart from the staff cloakroom. It was a small enough room as it was. She would have a word with Michaelis. See if something could be done.

She smiled to herself as she opened the door and began walking down the corridor towards the medical director's office. She was really beginning to feel like a career sister who wouldn't stand any nonsense from anybody. Like one of those dragons she remembered from her nursing training days. Twenty-eight years old she was, going on forty if she wasn't careful! But did it matter that she'd lost all interest in everything except work and her children? That's what she'd vowed to do after Patrick had died and that's what she'd achieved, wasn't it?

She tapped lightly on the door and pushed it open when she heard Michaelis call, 'Come in.

'Ah, Chloe. You got my message.'

Sara's fiancé, Michaelis, was a tall, dark, impressive-looking man. Since Sara had moved into his house, Chloe had noticed he'd smartened up his appearance considerably. Having got used to seeing him in casual clothes most of the time, it had come as a surprise to see him actually beginning to look like a medical director. Today he was wearing a smart lightweight linen suit, obviously new. Sara must have persuaded Michaelis to go over to Rhodes on a shopping spree!

Michaelis was smiling as he came from behind his desk to greet her.

'I'd like you to meet Dr Demetrius Petros, our new doctor. He specialises in obstetrics so you'll be working together a great deal, I imagine. Demetrius worked here at the hospital for a short time some years ago before he went to Australia. I've just been explaining to Demetrius that as the hospital has expanded since he was last here, the medical staff are expected to work wherever they're needed most, but someone with a specialisation such as his will be of more use in Obstetrics than, say, in—'

Michaelis broke off, a look of concern crossing his dark, distinctive features. 'Is something the matter, Chloe? You've gone very pale. Why don't you sit down here?'

Michaelis was reaching for the bottle of water on his desk, hastily pouring out a glass and holding it out towards her.

'It's the heat, the early morning rush to get to work,' she murmured between sips as her eyes remained riveted on the tall figure by the window. The sun streaming through the windows was dazzling her eyes.

It couldn't be. But the name was the same...

'Demetrius.' Chloe didn't at first realise she'd spoken as her lips formed the man's name. She barely recognised her own whispering, croaking voice.

The man came towards her, away from the glare of the sun. For a few seconds that seemed like an eternity he stood looking down at her without speaking. The dark, enigmatic eyes were giving nothing away. Only the rigid clenching and unclenching of his hands told her that he was remembering that other life they'd shared. And in a blinding flash, she realised that the ghostly premonition out there on the water had been leading up to this moment, preparing her for the shock of seeing Demetrius again.

Except that she wasn't in the least prepared. She'd assumed she would never ever see him again. She'd thought, when she'd come back to Ceres that there wasn't the remotest chance that—

'Hello, Chloe,' he said evenly. 'I had no idea you were the sister in charge of the surgical floor.'

'Obviously you didn't know.' Chloe's voice came out more loudly than she'd intended.

She was still in a state of shock, trying desperately to stop herself from trembling. Her hands felt cold and clammy. Her head was light, full of cotton wool, her thoughts and emotions utterly confused. She couldn't comprehend the awful irony of meeting up again with Demetrius like this in a professional situation, both of them knowing that they wouldn't have come here if they'd known the other would be there.

Michaelis, in his professional role of medical director, continued as if nothing was amiss. 'I was going to formally introduce you.'

His distinctive Greek accent was much more pronounced now, showing that he was disturbed by the uncertainty of the situation. 'Dr Demetrius Petros, this is Sister Chloe Metcalfe. Do I take it you've met before?'

The new doctor nodded his head, his eyes still holding

Chloe's gaze of dismay. 'We met before I went to Australia.'

The dismay she was feeling was her way of holding back her true emotions. She mustn't drop her guard. She couldn't give in to the feeling that if only Demetrius would lean forward and take her in his arms she would capitulate and everything would be as it had been before, in that idyllic time long ago.

She leaned back against the chair, wondering how she could have allowed such a wild, abandoned thought to enter her head. She'd vowed never to give in to a mad impulse ever again, and until this moment it hadn't been difficult.

'I suppose that was when you were here on holiday, before Demetrius went to Australia,' Michaelis said in a conversational tone. 'Let me give you both some coffee while you catch up on your news.'

'Yes, it was one summer…' Chloe began.

'Eight years ago,' Demetrius supplied, pulling a chair to the side of Demetrius's desk. He drank deeply from the coffee-cup which Michaelis had placed in front of him.

'I'd taken three months off from my nursing training so that I could spend the summer out here with my family. I remember I went back to England in the middle of September. I had to get back—to my nursing studies.'

Chloe felt her emotions churning at the memory of that fateful morning when she'd clung to the rails of the ferry as it had left Ceres harbour, her heart broken to be leaving behind the man she still loved in spite of the fact he'd rejected her.

'I gather you finished your nursing training as you intended,' Demetrius said, the hint of a frown on his dark, ruggedly handsome face.

'Dr Michaelis…'

The side door to the secretary's office had opened and the small, plump, middle-aged, immensely capable Panayota appeared carrying some letters.

'Oh, sorry, Dr Michaelis, I didn't realise…'

'That's OK, Panayota. I'll come into your office and we'll finish the letters together. There are one or two things I need to clarify with you.'

Michaelis seemed relieved to be able to escape the tense atmosphere of his office. He smiled reassuringly at Chloe and Demetrius before disappearing with his secretary.

The door closed. Demetrius stood up and moved over to the window. Shakily, Chloe followed him, partly because the sun was still dazzling her eyes as she watched him and partly because she wanted to see if she could be close to him in a professional situation. If she couldn't then the idea of them working together was a non-starter.

He hadn't changed much. A little thinner perhaps? And the hint of a few lines at the corners of his dark brown eyes. He must be thirty-four now, because he was six years older than she was. He'd removed the jacket of his dark grey suit. Underneath, his bright orange shirt, open at the neck, looked crumpled.

She stood by the window, half sitting on the sill so that her legs wouldn't collapse beneath her.

'Yes, I finished my nursing training.' Her voice was barely audible. She cleared her throat and started again in a firmer tone. 'I took my finals the following summer.'

Chloe looked out of the window at the busy harbour below as her thoughts returned to that difficult time. The twins' birth in June, returning to the hospital nursing school after a few weeks' maternity leave and taking her finals when the twins had been only six weeks old. She could remember distinctly the claustrophobic smell of the examination room. She hadn't wanted to be there. She'd been up half the night with the twins. Patrick had always slept like a log and because he'd worked in a very demanding teaching job, she'd known he'd needed his sleep.

It had been his first year of teaching English at the local comprehensive school and he'd always been tired. So Chloe had looked after the twins almost single-handedly. And because she'd still been breastfeeding the babies, she'd had to hurry home at the end of each exam session to be with them again.

From the harbour she heard the sound of the departing ferry. She could see the people holding onto the rails as they waved goodbye to their friends. Were any of them saying goodbye to their dreams, as she had done? She hoped not, for their sakes. She wouldn't wish on anybody the trauma she'd experienced since she'd left the island on that ferry eight years ago in September.

Demetrius took a step forward. 'I expect you passed your exams with flying colours. Best student in your year?'

She raised her eyes to his. 'No, nothing like that. I just…I just scraped through, actually. I had to resit one paper.'

Demetrius raised an eyebrow. 'You surprise me. I always thought you were something of a…how do you say it in English? A brain box? What happened? Didn't you study hard enough?'

'I had…I had a few distractions.'

'Ah, yes, your boyfriend.' Demetrius's tone was cold. 'I suppose you decided to get engaged to him.'

'Actually, we were married by the time I took my finals.'

'You were married?' Demetrius stared at her. 'Before your finals?'

'Yes, in the March before my finals,' she said, quickly.

Now was the time to tell Demetrius she was the mother

of twins. Now, before things got more complicated. But the shock of seeing him, the turmoil of her emotions…something was holding her back. She couldn't think straight any more. But it was mad of her to dither like this, totally uncharacteristic to hold back when sooner or later Demetrius would have to know the truth.

'Patrick and I saw no reason to delay our marriage,' she said quietly.

And every reason to get married. Patrick had managed to convince her, in spite of all the arguments she'd put forward to the contrary, that they had to be a married couple before the birth of the twins.

But still she couldn't bring herself to mention Rachel and Samantha.

'Are you in love with Patrick?' Demetrius said, a trace of bitterness creeping into his voice.

So he didn't know she was a widow. Chloe raised herself from the window-sill. 'Demetrius, stop quizzing me! We're both here to work and there's no need to…'

Her voice sounded more harsh than she'd intended. She was fighting back the tears. With a swift, impulsive movement, Demetrius reached forward and drew her against him, encircling her with his strong muscular arms.

'Ah, that's more like the Chloe I remember! So you haven't lost any of your fiery spirit after all.'

For a moment she leaned her head against his shoulder, revelling in the scent of his aftershave, the aura of virile masculinity pervading around him, the hardness of his muscular body…

What was she doing, allowing herself to drop her guard like this? She pulled herself away, standing back as she looked up into his expressive eyes. A slight, mocking smile had appeared on his sensual lips, those lips that had claimed hers so many times. Those lips that had promised her the earth but had finally betrayed her. She was trying so hard to remain sensible but she knew that if Demetrius were to take her in his arms again and kiss her, she would break all her resolutions.

'Demetrius, if we're to work together we've got to forget the past,' she said in a deliberately prim voice. 'I say "if" because at the moment I'm wondering how we're going to cope in a professional situation.'

Demetrius shrugged. 'Oh, you'll cope all right, Chloe. You always do. You won't let your emotions run away with you…like you did just now when I asked if you loved your husband. That was a one-off aberration for you. I doubt whether you'll behave in such an unguarded way again. I sense that deep down you're still a passionate woman but you've obviously learned to control yourself over the years. Maybe your husband makes you—'

'I have no husband,' she said quietly. 'Patrick was killed in a car crash six months after we were married.'

An expression of dismay crossed Demetrius's face. 'I'm so sorry. I didn't know. I wouldn't have been so thoughtless. Please, forgive me.'

Demetrius reached forward and gently took hold of Chloe's hand. It was a friendly gesture, made to comfort her. As he led her back to her chair by the desk he could feel her whole body trembling. Dear God, if only he'd known she'd been alone all those years. How different their life might have been!

As Demetrius poured out another cup of coffee for Chloe from the cafetière on the desk he found himself rearranging his ideas about Patrick, the man who'd stolen Chloe from him. He remembered when she'd first told him about the boyfriend back home.

They'd been childhood sweethearts, apparently, but their relationship had been going through a rough patch. Chloe had been wondering whether they should split up or not. The boyfriend had wanted their relationship to continue. When Chloe had said she wanted to take time out to think about it, he'd agreed that she should go to Ceres with her parents to sort out her feelings.

That was when Demetrius had met Chloe and they'd fallen in love. After a short time together, he'd honestly thought Chloe would stay with him on Ceres for ever. But, for some unknown reason, she'd returned to the boyfriend in England.

'Drink this, Chloe.' Demetrius handed her the cup before picking up his own.

She gave him a gentle smile. He felt a deep sensual desire stirring inside him as he saw that wistful little smile. He remembered it so well. She'd been so coy at times, teasing him along until they'd been in each other's arms. He remembered how she would mould her body against his, how they would fit together with every contour, every tiny—

'Demetrius, you're spilling your coffee!'

'Oops!' Demetrius grinned as Chloe leaned forward to mop the stain from his trouser leg with a tissue.

Mopping at the dark brown stain on the grey, textured cloth, Chloe became aware that she could feel the muscles of Demetrius's thigh contracting. The frisson of excitement that shot through her was sensually disturbing. She shouldn't be performing this seemingly innocent task in what had developed into an intimate situation. Quickly she pulled her hand away and leaned back in her chair, breathing deeply to regain her composure.

'You ought to soak that in cold water as soon as you can,' she said, resorting to her prim, no-nonsense voice, 'otherwise…'

Demetrius's eyes were twinkling as he stood up and

began to undo the top button of his trousers. 'Perhaps it would be better if I took them off now and—'

'Demetrius, no!'

Demetrius threw back his head and roared with laughter, that delicious appealing laugh that had always thrilled her.

'Only joking!' He sat down again, but pulled his chair closer to hers. 'I can't see why you should look so scandalised. After all…'

The door opened and Michaelis returned. 'I'm glad you two seem to have broken the ice. I heard Demetrius laughing just now and knew it was safe to come back again. What's the joke?'

'It's not really funny,' Chloe said, quickly. 'Demetrius spilled his coffee. I've suggested he go and change so that his trousers can be cleaned properly.'

'Panayota will fix you up with a pair of theatre pants if you like, Demetrius,' Michaelis said.

'Fine!' Demetrius said, in an easygoing voice.

Chloe, hardly daring to glance at him, saw that his face held that naughty-boy grin that he'd often worn when they'd been together. He'd always enjoyed winding her up!

Oh, why couldn't his personality have changed? If only he looked older, more set in his ways, a stuffy type of doctor she couldn't possibly fancy. Why had he remained exactly the same character that she'd fallen for during that fateful summer holiday, with such disastrous results?

The phone was ringing. A good time to escape. 'I've got to get back to my ward,' Chloe said quickly as she stood up.

'Wait a moment, Chloe!' Michaelis's hand was outstretched towards her as he listened to someone at the other end of the phone. 'Yes, right away.'

He put down the phone. 'There's been a car crash. A

young pregnant woman is just being transferred from the emergency department to Obstetrics. I've told them you'll be returning at once, Chloe.'

Demetrius stood up, his expression solemn and professional again. 'I'll come, too. I'd like to start work as soon as possible.'

'Thanks, Demetrius,' Michaelis said. 'I'm sure you'll be a great help to Chloe.'

Hurrying along beside Demetrius, Chloe forced herself to switch back to professional mode. The fact that Demetrius was here, at her side, after all these years was incredible. But for the moment she must think only of her emergency patient, a pregnant car crash victim. It would depend how advanced the pregnancy was and—

'Dr Demetrius!'

They both turned. Panayota was hurrying behind them, clutching a pair of green theatre trousers.

'These should fit you.'

'Thanks, Panayota,' Demetrius said, grinning as he held the trousers against him for a moment. 'Bit short but I don't mind showing my ankles. I'm sure Chloe will find me a quiet corner in which to change.'

'Of course, Doctor.' Chloe continued down the white-painted corridor, now some way ahead of Demetrius.

'Hey, wait for me, Chloe!'

Chloe felt a sensual shiver running through her as Demetrius put his hand on her arm. How on earth she was going to get through the next few hours she simply didn't know! She coped with shock and trauma every day of her life but today was different. Today she had to put herself on autopilot, with no emotional considerations whatsoever, otherwise she'd be useless in the emergency situation ahead of her.

They climbed the steps to the first floor. Everyone Chloe

met greeted her with, '*Kali mera*, good morning, Chloe.'
It was good to be part of such a friendly, efficient team.

'Michaelis told me you're in charge of the whole of this
floor, Chloe. Quite a responsible job.'

'I mostly work in Obstetrics but, yes, I have overall
charge of the other wards,' Chloe explained.

'Will you show me around later?'

'I'll try, but if I'm tied up, please, feel free to make
yourself known to everybody,' Chloe said. 'There's a sister
or staff nurse in each ward who will be only too pleased
to help you.'

Walking along the corridor, catching glimpses of the
various wards—surgical, orthopaedic and paediatric—she
felt a surge of pride that she should be so involved in this
excellent hospital.

'It's changed so much since I was working here,'
Demetrius said. 'Since the building was expanded you've
had to get a lot more staff. I can't believe it's the same
hospital I knew.'

Turning in through the swing doors that led to the obstetrics and gynaecology department, Chloe indicated one
of the bathrooms. 'You can change in there, Demetrius.'

She found that one of the doctors and a staff nurse were
attending to the new patient in a side ward.

'Ah, Chloe, glad you're here.' Andonis, a very capable
doctor, was leaning over the patient. 'I'm needed in the
delivery suite, but I don't like to leave the patient until—'

'I'll take over from you, Andonis,' Demetrius said, hurrying in through the door.

Chloe suppressed a smile as she saw the bizarre outfit
he was wearing. The green theatre pants clashed dreadfully
with his bright orange shirt. So long as he was a good
obstetrician she didn't mind what he was wearing. And the
fact that he looked as if he'd stepped off the stage in a

pantomime didn't in any way detract from the fact that he was still the most handsome, desirable man she'd ever known.

'Demetrius!' Andonis was pumping his hand. 'When did you get back? I thought you were permanently settled in Australia. Got to go. Catch you later.'

The two men had been speaking in Greek. Chloe was glad that her knowledge of the language had improved while she'd been working here to the point that she could understand most of what was said and converse fluently when required.

But looking down at her patient, she knew she wouldn't need her Greek here. The ashen-faced, blonde young woman stared up at Chloe with troubled blue eyes.

'I'm Fiona, Sister. Nobody's told me if I'm going to lose my baby.'

'We'll do everything we can to prevent that happening, Fiona,' Chloe said, soothingly taking hold of the patient's hand.

It was cold and clammy. Shock affected patients in different ways. Chloe glanced at the notes Andonis had made. Pulse, respiration and blood pressure all too high. Thirty weeks pregnant. A crucial time. She handed the notes across the bed to Demetrius.

'Are you having any pain, Fiona?' Demetrius asked.

'No, I hit my head on the car roof but I didn't black out.'

'You're thirty weeks pregnant?'

'Yes. I can feel him kicking me now, but I don't think he's happy.'

'Well, it's a good sign if he's kicking,' Chloe said.

'He's going to be a footballer,' Fiona told them. 'Dave—that's my husband, he's just gone out for a breath of air—watched him on the last scan I had last month and he can tell he's got footballer's legs.'

Demetrius smiled. 'Sister Chloe will arrange for you to have another scan today. But first I'd like to examine you.'

Chloe rolled back the sheet, leaving a small blanket to cover her patient. Demetrius scrubbed up at the sink in the corner of the room before putting on the gloves Chloe handed to him.

Whilst he was examining Fiona she talked about what had happened when the car had crashed. It transpired that her husband had been driving down the steep hill from the upper town to the harbour when another car had rounded the corner slightly over on their side of the narrow road. Dave had steered their car out of the way but it had turned over in the ditch and Fiona had been jerked onto her side.

'Fortunately I was wearing my seat belt but it didn't half pull against my tummy. Tommy, that's the name we've given our baby, was absolutely still for a bit and I was so worried. But when we got to the hospital, he livened up for a bit, bless him!'

Fiona patted her abdomen and raised her head from the pillow so that she could look at Demetrius. 'So what do you think, Doctor?'

Demetrius straightened up, peeling off his gloves as he stood looking down at Fiona, a sympathetic expression on his face.

'Well, no harm seems to have been done to Tommy. But we'll need to keep you in for a while just to be sure.'

Demetrius turned to look at Chloe. 'We need round-the-clock monitoring of the foetal heartbeat, Chloe, along with all the routine antenatal checks. Blood pressure is too high so we'll have to keep an eye on that and take steps to bring it down if it gets any higher. Hopefully, our patient's condition will improve over the next few days and then she'll be able to be discharged.'

'Few days!' Fiona clutched at the sheet. 'I'm only here for a couple of weeks. What about my holiday?'

'Fiona, we have to be sure. When's your flight home?'

'In ten days. I'll be OK by then, won't I?'

Demetrius patted Fiona's hand. 'If you do what Chloe tells you. For the moment, I want you to stay here on full bed rest.'

Fiona was still muttering about wanting to get out of hospital when Demetrius and Chloe left her.

'I always like to err on the side of caution,' Demetrius said, as he followed Chloe into her office. 'Where pregnant women and babies are concerned, it's best not to take any chances.'

Chloe nodded. 'I agree with you there. I'll get that ultrasound scan organised.'

As she picked up the phone, Demetrius held out his hand to detain her. 'Just a moment, before you go all bossy and professional on me again.'

Chloe gave him a shy smile, unaware how the sight of that smile was playing havoc with Demetrius's emotions.

'How can I help you, Doctor?'

'I just thought…that is, I was wondering if we could have a drink together this evening when we go off duty. Just for old times' sake. You can say no if you feel that—'

'No…I mean, yes, I'd like to have a drink with you. The only thing is…'

Chloe took a deep breath. Now was the moment she was going to tell him. But only so much. Not the real truth.

'It will have to be a quick drink because I want to get home to my children.'

Complete disbelief appeared on Demetrius's face. 'Children? You have children? But you said you were only married for six months.'

'Long enough for me to have twins,' she said defensively.

'Twins! I'm amazed!' Demetrius still looked shell-shocked as he stared down at her. Suddenly he seemed to recover his composure. 'What are they—girls, boys? How old are they?'

'Two girls, aged seven…well, nearly eight.'

She tried desperately to hide her anxiety as she saw Demetrius's shocked expression change. Why had she admitted they were nearly eight? Was Demetrius doing rapid mathematical calculations now? If she'd simply said they were seven…

'I see.' Demetrius stood quite still, staring down at her with troubled eyes.

No, you don't see! But I can't tell you any more. Not for the moment. Not when I've managed to keep the secret for so long.

A light was flashing on her desk. Over the intercom came the message that a doctor was needed in the delivery room.

'I'm on my way,' Demetrius responded immediately, as he dashed out of Chloe's office.

Chloe stared after him. How was she going to handle the situation of Demetrius and the twins? How, after all these years when she'd been lulled into a false sense of security, was she going to cope?

Demetrius had a right to know the twins were his. She remembered how she'd gone back to England, devastated that Demetrius had made it clear he didn't want her to stay. She'd known she hadn't wanted to return to the old life and resume her relationship with Patrick. She'd already decided not to go back to Patrick even before she met

Demetrius. And their affair had simply convinced her that she'd made the right decision.

Patrick had reluctantly accepted the situation, and Chloe had felt fortunate that they'd remained very close friends. And when the bombshell had dropped and Chloe had discovered she was pregnant, Patrick had become her rock.

Even though he'd known she only loved him as a friend, Patrick had wanted Chloe to marry him. Their families hadn't known about the split, and Patrick had used all his powers of persuasion on Chloe to get married and raise the baby as his.

Perhaps naïvely, Chloe had agreed. At the time, it had seemed the best thing to do. And now she had to face the consequences of her actions all those years ago.

CHAPTER TWO

As SHE finished giving her report, Chloe handed over the ward keys to Staff Nurse Katerina who'd just come on duty. She liked her capable second in command very much. Brought up in Australia by Greek-Australian parents, she was extremely good at her work here in the hospital. Apart from her Greek grandmother and the other relatives who still lived on the island, most other people called Katerina Kate.

'Thanks, Chloe,' Kate said, as she put the keys in the pocket of her white uniform dress. 'Sounds like you had a busy day.'

'Hasn't been a moment's peace.' Chloe put her hand to her head as she felt her little white cap wobbling. One of the pins fell down onto the desk. 'No point fixing this back again now I'm going off duty.' She put the cap on her desk. 'I won't be sorry to go off duty this evening. It's been a long day.'

'Well, don't worry any more. I'm in charge now, so take it easy. I'll run along and check on Fiona.' Kate paused by the door. 'You say the ultrasound was normal?'

'As far as we could make out, but keep an eye on that foetal heartbeat.'

As the door closed, Chloe kicked off her shoes and wiggled her toes under the desk. Apprehensive thoughts about the impending evening came rushing into her head. Demetrius hadn't been back to discuss what time they should meet for that drink. Well, she wasn't going to hang around waiting. She shouldn't have agreed to go for a drink, anyway. It was just asking for trouble. Now he knew she had the twins he would be sure to start quizzing her again about when they were actually born.

What on earth had she let herself in for? she wondered as, having removed her cap, she felt wisps of hair falling over her face. Quickly she tugged the rest of the pins and clips from the knot at the nape of her neck and let her hair come tumbling down.

Phew, that was better! Chloe ran a hand through her tousled hair and leaned back against the chair. She'd worked with Demetrius for part of the morning in the delivery room and had been very impressed by his skills and experience. Yes, he was going to be a great asset to the department. There shouldn't be a problem with their professional life, provided she could keep a hold on her emotions. And they wouldn't be working together all the time. There were times when Demetrius would be needed elsewhere, like this afternoon when he'd been called down to the emergency department. Since then she'd lost track of him.

She still had no idea how she was going to tackle the problem of the twins. She'd never taken anyone into her confidence. Even at her most desperate moments, when she'd longed to confide in one of her sisters or her mother, she'd felt it kinder to keep quiet. Especially with her mother. She was sure Pam would be devastated if she knew the truth. Patrick had been her mother's godson, the son of one of her closest friends, and she'd known him since he was a baby.

Now, with Anthony, her father, the situation was somehow different. She'd often wondered if he had an inkling about the truth. There was something about his expression when he looked at her sometimes. He was always stressing the fact that the twins' dark hair was just like his mother's had been before it had gone grey. Just like his own brown hair only darker, he would say with a kind of forced emphasis that worried Chloe.

She wouldn't put it past her retired surgeon father to have deduced that two and two made four! But he was such a gentleman. Even with his own daughters he never pried into their affairs. He was always there to give advice if it was asked for but never offered it when it wasn't wanted.

'Ah, there you are!' Demetrius stood in the doorway. 'I did knock but you didn't hear me. You look as if you're off duty at last. So, how about this drink? Not changed your mind, I hope.'

Chloe ran a hand through her tousled hair, pushing it back over her ears.

'Of course I haven't changed my mind.' Chloe stood up. 'Give me five minutes to change and I'll meet you in the reception area. But, like I said, I can't stay long.'

'I know, you've got to get back to the twins.'

She glanced across the room at him but his expression was totally impassive.

The phone was ringing. Automatically, she picked it up, forgetting that she was supposed to be off duty and that Kate was technically in charge.

'Chloe!' It was Sara's voice.

'Hi, Sara. What can I do for you?'

'Michaelis and I wondered if you'd like a lift home. Mum's asked us over for dinner. She wants to get on with the wedding plans.'

'Yes, I would like a lift. Good thing you phoned. I've only just remembered I forgot to phone Manolis, so he'll take it I don't need him to pick me up this evening. The only thing is…' She glanced nervously across at Demetrius who was pretending not to listen in. 'I've promised to have a drink with the new doctor and—'

'You mean Demetrius?' Sara's excited voice could be heard clearly over the phone. 'He's gorgeous, Chloe! He came down to work here in the emergency department this afternoon and—'

'Actually, he's here with me now, Sara, so I'd better go. Would you and Michaelis like to join us for a drink before we—'

'Of course! Be a pleasure.'

'Meet us in Reception in ten minutes?'

'You're on, Sis!'

Chloe glanced across the room at Demetrius, who was trying to control the amused smile that was playing on his lips.

'That was my sister Sara,' she said, unnecessarily.

'We worked together this afternoon but, then, I think she told you that didn't she? I was trying not to listen but she's got a distinctive voice, your sister.'

Chloe smiled. 'Distinctive as in loud. She's so happy since she moved in with Michaelis that she positively bubbles over all the time. This time last year she was so quiet and subdued but now...'

'Love can completely change a person's character, can't it?' Demetrius's voice was deep and husky and his eyes held her gaze.

She looked down at the desk, moving aside a pile of case notes, straightening the pens and pencils on the little carved wooden tray.

'It's certainly changed Sara,' Chloe said evenly, trying desperately to remain objective. She stood up. 'We've got ten minutes, Demetrius, and I need to change. I see you've managed to change out of those awful theatre pants.'

Demetrius laughed. 'They didn't quite go with my shirt,

did they? One of the nurses in Emergency cleaned the coffee stain from my trousers. Pretty good job, eh?'

'Excellent.' She made for the door.

Demetrius was still standing in the doorway, one hand on the doorpost blocking her way.

She tried to duck under his arm, but he put one hand on her waist and drew her towards him. With his other hand he gently touched the tousled strands of her hair, lightly running his fingers through it in the way she remembered he'd so often done in their brief time together. It had often been the precursor to something more exciting, a situation where they would cling to each other before frantically searching for somewhere where they could consummate their wildly disturbing love.

Chloe took a deep breath as she tried to remain in control of her turbulent emotions. She mustn't give way to the tremors of passion that were running through her. Someone might see them in this compromising position. Someone might jump to conclusions.

'Demetrius…'

'It's OK,' he said gently. 'I'm not going to compromise your honour. Not here anyway. I simply wanted to say that you don't need to worry I'll say something I shouldn't in front of your sister. We kept our affair secret before. No reason why—'

'Demetrius, that was all in the past. Everything has changed. I've moved on and—'

'I can see that. But you're deluding yourself. Nothing has changed.'

Looking up into his eyes, she knew he was speaking the truth. She was still deeply in love. And how was she going to handle that? How would Demetrius feel about the way she'd deprived him of nearly eight years of his daughters' lives? Working with him this morning in the delivery room, she'd seen how he adored babies. She knew he would have made a wonderful father if only she'd…

'Come on, let's get a move on,' he said, brusquely. 'I'll go ahead and meet Sara and Michaelis while you change.'

Sara was looking as radiant as ever when Chloe, her hastily combed hair swinging madly from side to side, arrived in Reception. She smoothed down her cotton skirt, fastening the last button of her blouse as she smiled at her petite, brown-haired sister.

Sara took after their father in looks, but she was the only sister not to have inherited his long legs. Chloe and Francesca, her elder sister, had their petite mother's blonde hair but they were tall, like their father.

'We've decided on that taverna at the corner of the harbour,' Michaelis told Chloe. 'You know, the one that's built on that piece of land that juts out into the sea, just before you turn off to go round to Nimborio. I've got the four-wheel-drive out front, so let's go.'

Sara took the passenger seat next to Michaelis. Demetrius opened the back door and helped Chloe inside. She was glad that the other three kept up a flowing conversation as they drove round the harbour because she didn't feel like talking. There was too much to think about.

She looked out of the window at the crowded harbour. The start of another evening on Ceres. The excited anticipation of a relaxing few hours in the company of good friends. Tourists mingled with the people who lived on the island. Barmen were serving drinks, music could be heard from the speakers inside the tavernas. People were sitting out on the smart yachts tied up on the quayside, sipping cocktails before they decided where they would have dinner.

Eight years ago, if she'd been sitting here with

Demetrius by her side in the back of the car, she would have been the happiest girl in the world. But she couldn't go back to those halcyon days. She had to go forward and face her responsibilities.

She shivered.

Demetrius reached across and took hold of her hand. 'You can't be cold, Chloe. Are you OK?'

'Tired, that's all,' she said quietly, desperately aware that Michaelis was watching them in his rear-view mirror. Demetrius's large, capable hand enclosing hers was comforting. Comforting, yes, but impossibly disturbing. She mustn't allow herself to relax. Mustn't give the show away in front of Sara and Michaelis. Mustn't give Demetrius the impression that she wanted them to carry on where they'd left off. He'd rejected her once and once bitten, twice shy. She wasn't going to let him break her heart again.

The taverna on the corner of the harbour was quieter than the ones in the centre of Ceres town. Chloe looked out across the water and marvelled as she always did at the superb view of the hillside on the other side of the bay. Twinkling lights were beginning to appear in the pastel-coloured houses that spilled down towards the water.

The little green seven-o'clock bus was trundling its way up the road to Chorio, the upper town where Demetrius had lived when she'd first known him. She wondered fleetingly where he lived now. Having lived in Australia, he'd probably sold that lovely house that she'd come to regard as home.

The bus still ran on the hour as it had done that fateful summer. On the hour or sometimes ten minutes early, especially at lunchtime when the driver was in a hurry to have his midday break. But on the sleepy island of Ceres, time was unimportant. Close to their table by the water, she could see the silver scales of the fish swimming by, drawn to the surface by the overhead lights on the terrace of the taverna.

'Ouzo, Michaelis?' Demetrius asked as the waiter approached.

Michaelis nodded, adding in Greek that he'd also like a glass of water because he was driving. *'Ena potiri nero, parakalor.'*

'And the ladies?' Demetrius asked.

'Let's share a small bottle of retsina,' Sara suggested.

'Fine!' Chloe smiled. She was beginning to relax. Being close to the sea always soothed her. She watched the fish swimming around in circles. Demetrius picked up a piece of bread that had been left on the next table and threw some crumbs into the water. The fish became more and more excited as they nibbled at the bread.

The waiter set the drinks down on the table, opening the small bottle of retsina and pouring out two glasses for Sara and Chloe. There was also a plate of black olives with some feta cheese. Chloe took a sip from her glass before chewing an olive. The strong, bitter taste made her feel nostalgic again. She looked across at Demetrius and saw that he was watching her.

'I'm glad I came back to the island,' he said slowly. 'Don't know how I could stay away so long. Especially when—'

'What made you come back to Ceres?' Chloe broke in, fearful that Demetrius would reveal too much about their shared past.

'Simply got homesick. And my marriage had broken up so there was no reason for me to stay in Australia.'

'I didn't know you were married,' Chloe said quietly.

'There's a lot you don't know about me, Chloe.' Demetrius poured water into his glass of ouzo and the liquid clouded. He took a long drink before putting his glass down. 'Just as there's a lot I don't know about you.'

Michaelis was watching them. 'You've told me you met before but—'

'It was all a long time ago,' Chloe said hastily. 'I was only twenty. We saw each other a few times but lost touch after I went back to finish my nursing training.'

Sara was looking puzzled. 'Was that one of the years when I went on an exchange visit to France, Chloe?'

A mobile phone started ringing. Sara rummaged in her shoulder-bag.

'I think it must have been,' Chloe said, as her sister searched for the shrilling phone.

'I missed a few of the family holidays didn't I? Hi, Mum.' Sara was smiling as she answered the phone. 'We're on our way... No, we stopped off for a drink... Chloe's with us and Demetrius, the new doctor... Well, I'll ask him.'

Sara looked at Demetrius. 'Mum says she and Dad would like to meet you, Demetrius.'

Michaelis leaned towards Demetrius. 'Sara's father is Anthony Metcalfe, the famous surgeon. Brilliant man! I was a student of Professor Metcalfe for a short while in England. Learned a lot. You ought to meet him.'

Demetrius took a deep breath as he reviewed the situation. This wasn't the time to admit that he'd met Anthony Metcalfe eight years ago and the meeting hadn't gone all that smoothly.

'I'm not sure whether—'

'Oh, come on, Demetrius!' Sara said. 'It's only a family supper, not a full-scale dinner party. And you've got to eat, haven't you?'

Perhaps he could bluff it out. Chloe's father had all the

hallmarks of a real gentleman. He wouldn't start bringing up the past…or would he?

'Well, if you're sure I'm not imposing, I'll—'

Sara smiled. 'Demetrius says he'd be delighted to join us, Mum. Be with you in a few minutes.'

'Well, that's settled, then,' Michaelis said, knocking back the remains of his drink. 'Drink up and we'll be on our way.'

Demetrius stood at the bottom of the path that led up to the Metcalfes' house. He remembered how nervous he'd been the last time. He felt ten times more nervous now! He wondered if Professor Metcalfe had ever told Chloe about their heated discussion. He would soon find out.

Pam Metcalfe came out onto the terrace to watch as the four of them walked up the path. Demetrius looked up at the petite, blonde-haired, pretty woman who was Chloe's mother and thought what a striking appearance she had. The sort of woman who would stand out in a crowd, she was also the kind of person you wouldn't want to have a dispute with. On either side of her was a beautiful little girl with dark brown hair. One was wearing pink pyjamas, the other blue. Apart from that, there was no way of telling them apart. Demetrius felt a lump rising in his throat. These could so easily have been his little daughters if only…

A blinding flash of revelation shot through him like an electric current. How old had Chloe said the twins were? Nearly eight? How nearly was nearly? This month, next month…? Did that mean…?

They had finished climbing the stairs that led to the terrace. The little girls broke away from their grandmother. With a whoop of excitement they shot forward to fling their arms around their mother. Chloe was kneeling down, revelling in the feeling of those two pairs of loving arms around her neck.

'Mummy, Mummy, I drew you a picture at school,' the girl in pink was saying. 'Do you want to come and see it?'

'And I caught a fish with Grandpa. A big fish…this long…'

Demetrius watched as the blue-clad arms extended to full length. The brown-haired heads close to their mother's blonde hair were almost too much for him to take. He had to know! He had to find out exactly how old they were. But he'd have to be subtle. No one must suspect that he'd divined the impossible truth.

If indeed it was the truth.

'And you must be Demetrius.' Pam Metcalfe was standing in front of him, holding out her hand.

'How do you do, Mrs Metcalfe?'

'Oh, please, call me Pam… Ah, here's my husband. Darling, this is Dr Demetrius Petros…'

'I know.'

The distinguished surgeon was almost as tall as Demetrius. The two men confronted each other, eyeball to eyeball, and for a few seconds there was silence. Then Anthony Metcalfe held out his hand towards Demetrius.

'You must call me Anthony. It's nice to meet you, Demetrius. How are you getting on at the hospital?'

Demetrius almost sighed with relief as he shook the surgeon's hand. So Chloe's father was going to go along with the charade, pretending they had never met. No one would know about that heated argument they'd had just before Chloe had gone back to her prospective fiancé.

Demetrius swallowed hard. 'I'm very impressed with the hospital, sir…er, Anthony. It's an extremely well-organised place. Runs very efficiently.'

Anthony smiled. 'We're very proud of our hospital here on Ceres. I say "our" because now that Pam and I live here permanently I feel I'm very much part of the community. We've been coming here for years on holiday, of course. I expect our paths must have crossed at some point, Demetrius. It's a small island.'

'Yes, it is very small, isn't it?' Demetrius said quickly, thanking his lucky stars that Anthony wasn't about to blow the whistle on him. His admiration for Chloe's father was growing by the minute. He hadn't exactly disliked Professor Metcalfe on that previous occasion. He'd been in awe of him and he hadn't found him easy to talk to. But then there had been so much at stake. And in the end, in spite of all his efforts, he'd been the loser.

'You haven't met my granddaughters, have you, Demetrius? Chloe, bring the girls over here.'

Chloe, with a child clinging to each hand, approached them. Demetrius could see that she was almost reluctant to leave the other side of the room. He held his breath. Oh, they were lovely little girls! They were adorable! They were everything he would have wished for if only…

Chloe was standing in front of him now. He gazed down at the beautiful children.

'Demetrius, this is Samantha and this is Rachel.'

Demetrius knelt down so that he could be at eye level with the girls. Samantha watched him, her face solemn and enquiring, whereas Rachel's face broke into a mischievous grin as she reached forward to touch his thick dark hair.

'You've got a lot of hair,' Rachel said, with both hands now on Demetrius's head. 'A lot more than Grandpa. Why don't you grow a beard? I like beards. Manolis has got a beard and he has to cut it with some scissors and Maria says it makes a mess of her kitchen so she turns him out into the garden and—'

'Ow!' Demetrius winced as the playful little fingers tweaked a strand of his hair.

'Rachel, be careful, darling,' Chloe said, drawing her daughter against her side.

'Sorry. I didn't mean—'

'That's OK, Rachel.' Demetrius was smiling as he pulled himself back to his full height. He reached down and patted the little girl's head. 'You've got lovely hair.'

'It's dark like my mother's was,' Anthony said. 'And I had hair of a similar colour before I went grey. Not quite so dark perhaps, but it was brown as opposed to blonde like Chloe's. Chloe takes after her mother.'

Chloe held her breath. Why did her father have to use that defensive tone when he talked about the twins' hair? Looking at them now, standing next to Demetrius, she had to suppress a shiver. The dark hair, the strong pearly white teeth and the striking bone structure. Their skin, bronzed by the sun, held the same olive sheen. The dark eyes were the same. The mischievous grin on Rachel's face was identical to the one she'd seen so many times when Demetrius had been in a playful mood.

Reluctantly, she raised her eyes to look at him and saw he was gazing at her with an expression that held happiness and pain. His dark eyes were moist with unshed tears. He knew! Of course he knew. He'd divined the secret she'd promised to keep since the twins' birth.

Demetrius averted his eyes and looked down once more at the twins. Unbidden, Rachel had moved away from her mother and sister and taken hold of Demetrius's hand. She was staring up at him, as if trying to memorise his face.

'You're very tall, Demetrius. Taller than Grandpa. How did you get to be so tall? I'd like to be tall when I'm a big lady. Did you have to eat a lot of food?'

'I always ate everything on my plate,' Demetrius said

solemnly. 'And I always did everything my mother told me to do.'

Rachel gave a tinkling girlish laugh. 'I bet you didn't! Nobody ever does that. We don't, do we, Samantha?'

Samantha looked uncertain. The quieter of the two, she was rather overawed by the newcomer. He looked pleasant enough but she preferred to be with people she knew.

'Which one of you is the elder?' Demetrius asked.

'I am,' Samantha said quietly. 'Mum says I was born ten minutes before Rachel.'

'That's not very much, is it?' Rachel said. 'And we're both the same size, aren't we? You don't grow very much in ten minutes, do you?'

The little pink-pyjama-clad girl broke away from Demetrius and went to stand with her back against her sister. 'Look at our heads, Demetrius. Are we still the same height? Mum measures us and puts marks on our bedroom wall and there's never any difference.'

'Yes, you're both exactly the same,' Demetrius told them as he placed his hands on both heads.

'It's time for bed, girls,' Chloe said gently, kneeling down to put her arms around her daughters so that she could cuddle them against her.

'Oh, please, let us stay up for grown-up supper!' Rachel pleaded. 'We'll be really good. It's hours since we ate our own supper in the kitchen and I'm starving again. Besides, I need to eat lots so I can grow up to be tall like Demetrius.'

Chloe's eyes were drawn magnetically towards Demetrius. His expression had softened. He was no longer looking upset. He was actually enjoying being with the twins now. Especially, it seemed, with the precocious Rachel who could be something of a handful when they had dinner parties. Usually, their guests couldn't wait for the little girl to be whisked away to bed. But, then, Demetrius must have come to the obvious conclusion and be feeling the first pangs of paternal love.

Chloe smiled at her daughters. 'Well, if you're very good, you can stay up for the first course, but then—'

'Cool!' Rachel began, jumping up and down excitedly.

Everybody was now gravitating towards the terrace to watch the sunset. Small tables had been set near the crenellated wall that overlooked the sea. Manolis, circulating amongst them, was topping up glasses with champagne.

Chloe, detaching herself from the others, walked over to the terrace wall and looked out across the water. The sun was sinking behind the hill, its fiery crimson glow casting an ethereal blaze of colour over the sparse grass and the dry brown earth. The water in front of her was illuminated with the orange and red colours of the sun. How beautiful this island was! She loved living here. It was a perfect place to live if only…

She turned as she heard the chattering sound of her daughters coming nearer. Demetrius, now with a twin each side of him, was making his way over the ancient Greek mosaic cobblestones of the terrace. Oh, how right it all looked for Demetrius to be claimed by his daughters like that!

But how wrong it was in the realistic situation of the life they were all leading. If only they could capture this perfect moment and not go forward. Chloe would have liked all of them to be frozen in time, the twins enjoying their time with Demetrius, who in turn was obviously besotted by them. No questions would be asked, especially by Demetrius.

But she was wishing for the moon! She looked up and saw the pale glow of the moon taking over from the sun.

You had to live in the real world, not on some perfect planet where problems didn't exist.

'Mummy, Demetrius used to live in Australia,' Rachel said excitedly. 'It's on the other side of the world but he says he didn't have to stand on his head.'

'I knew they didn't stand on their heads,' Samantha said solemnly. 'The Australians walk with their feet like we do.'

The twins broke away, their attention suddenly diverted by the sight of a plate of Maria's temptingly delicious tiropita, the Greek cheese pie, which had been cut into bite-size pieces. They both perched themselves on chairs at a nearby table.

Demetrius was now standing close behind Chloe as she looked out once more across the water. The sun had disappeared behind the hill but the rainbow effect of its multicoloured rays was lighting up the sky with iridescent shades of pink and blue that were reflected in the sea below.

'What lovely children you have, Chloe,' Demetrius said, his voice husky with emotion.

She stood quite still as she felt his hand on the small of her back. If she turned round now she would be, oh, so close. She could cling to him and ask to be forgiven for robbing him of the joys of watching the twins grow from beautiful babies into fascinating little girls. She glanced sideways across the terrace. Her father was watching them. He turned away.

'I'm glad you think the children are lovely, Demetrius,' she said carefully. 'I think they're wonderful, of course, but some people find them a bit of a handful, especially in the evening when everyone is tired and—'

'I like being with them.' Demetrius moved to stand beside her, one hand on the low wall. He took a sip from his glass before setting it down on a nearby table. 'You've done a great job, bringing them up by yourself. How old were they when your husband died?'

His bland, enigmatic expression was giving nothing away. Perhaps, by some miracle, he hadn't surmised...but, no, he must have guessed by now.

'The twins were three months old,' Chloe said, hating the way her voice trembled when she spoke.

'When is their birthday, Chloe?'

Demetrius's patient, seemingly understanding tone was driving a stake through her heart. He knew and yet, like a cat tormenting a mouse, he was keeping up the pretence.

She cleared her throat. 'They'll be eight on the twelfth of June. It's only just over a week to the girls' birthday. I'll have to start making plans. They'll want to invite half the school but I'll try to limit it to about twenty. We'll have to—'

'Chloe!' He placed one hand on the side of her face and gently smoothed back a lock of hair that had escaped from behind her ear.

'That's better. I couldn't see your face when you were speaking,' he said, his calm tone belying the fact that a major crisis in their life was taking place. 'I expect you're going to be very busy, organising this birthday party. It must be difficult, being a single parent.'

Their eyes met. All Chloe's doubts disappeared. She would have to confess, explain exactly why she was forced to go along with her life in the way she did.

'Demetrius, we've got to talk, but not here.'

'What is there to talk about?' he asked in a pseudo-innocent voice.

'Supper's ready,' Pam announced, coming through from the sitting room to stand in the centre of the open French windows. 'If you'd all like to come to the dining room we'll—'

'I want to sit next to Demetrius!' Rachel said, rushing up to clasp him by the hand.

'So do I,' Samantha said, taking the other hand.

'You can sit either side of Demetrius,' Pam told them. 'Don't worry, Demetrius. It's only for the first course. When they go up to bed you'll be able to have some peace.'

'I enjoy being with them,' Demetrius said calmly, as they all went down the stairs to the dining room.

'Do you have children of your own, Demetrius?' Pam asked.

Chloe, walking behind them, held her breath as she waited for the answer.

'My wife and I are divorced,' Demetrius said quietly. 'We didn't have any children.'

'Oh, I'm so sorry,' Pam said. 'You seem such a natural with children. I expect it's something to do with your medical training. Though not all doctors are good with children. During my own nursing career I met some doctors who couldn't stand them. I met my husband when we were working in the same hospital.'

'Did you really? How interesting!'

Chloe smiled as she listened to her mother chattering on about their whirlwind romance, working together in Theatre, Anthony asking her to go out with him at the end of a long operation when she'd been so in awe of him she'd dropped the sterile forceps he'd asked her to hand him and he'd shouted at her. She'd heard it all before, but it was a story that newcomers to the house always found fascinating.

'So I was hooked for life,' Anthony said, reaching the round table and beginning to light the candles. 'Pam wanted to put place names out on the table tonight but I pointed out that it wasn't a dinner party, just a family supper…with the addition of Demetrius, of course. Come and sit next to me, Demetrius.'

'Demetrius has promised the girls they can sit either side of him, Anthony,' Pam said. 'So for the first course you'll have Rachel next to you. Then when she goes to bed Demetrius can move up a place.'

When they were all seated, Chloe looked round the table. She was glad they were having supper at the round family table instead of erecting the long, large, social-occasion one. It made the atmosphere so much more intimate. Her father had insisted she sit next to him. This was one occasion when she would have preferred not to be too close to Anthony and his all-seeing eyes.

Further round the table, Demetrius was listening to Rachel's continuous chatter. On his other side, Samantha was very quiet. Her eyelids were drooping and she looked as if her head would fall into the spinach soup before long.

'Would you like me to take you up to bed, Samantha?' Chloe asked gently.

Samantha shook her head. 'Not until Rachel comes with me.'

'She's fine!' Anthony turned to reassure Chloe. 'Let her stay and enjoy the fun.' He lowered his voice. 'Are you all right, Chloe?'

Chloe nodded. 'Of course. I'm a bit tired that's all. And hungry. Maria's spinach soup is delicious. I didn't have much time for lunch. Delivering babies is a very unpredictable job.'

'Tell me about it!' her father said. 'I remember one time when I was a junior house surgeon, there was this patient who swore blind she couldn't possibly be pregnant. The size of a house she was when she was brought in with abdominal pains. I remember I was starving and just about to go for my supper. All I wanted was to get the delivery over with. Well, I couldn't convince this patient she was having a baby until I actually handed her the screaming, red-faced little bundle of evidence.'

'Why did the lady say she wasn't having a baby when she was, Grandpa?' Samantha asked, suddenly coming out of her soporific state to poise her soup-coated spoon over the starched white tablecloth.

'She probably wasn't ready enough to have the baby,' Rachel said knowledgeably. 'She hadn't had time to go to the shops to buy the nappies and stuff like that. So she wanted Grandpa to keep the baby in her tummy a bit longer. Why didn't you do that, Grandpa?'

With difficulty, holding back his amusement, Professor Metcalfe adopted his tried and tested let's-be-patient-with-the-student expression. 'Well, it's not as easy as that, Rachel. Babies have minds of their own and if they think it's time to come into the world, they'll jolly well arrive whether you're ready for them or not.'

'But how did the baby get in the mummy's tummy in the first place, Grandpa?' Rachel asked.

Anthony looked around the table as if searching for someone to help him out.

'The daddy had planted a seed in the mummy,' Demetrius said solemnly. 'And it grew and grew until it became a baby big enough to live outside the mummy's tummy.'

Chloe swallowed the lump in her throat as she watched the twins, enraptured by Demetrius's attention.

'Does it hurt the mummy when the daddy plants the seed in her tummy?' Rachel asked, wide-eyed with interest.

Demetrius glanced at Chloe for help.

Chloe hesitated, considering her words carefully. One day her daughters would grow up and be ready to experience all of this at first hand so she must be truthful.

'Actually…' Chloe paused to take a deep breath. 'Actually, it doesn't hurt when the daddy plants the seed in the mummy. It's rather pleasant.'

It was at this point that Samantha, leaning sleepily sideways towards Demetrius, dropped her sticky spoon onto his trouser leg.

Chloe got up from the table to move round behind her daughter. 'I'm so sorry Demetrius. Your trousers—again!'

Their eyes met and Demetrius smiled. 'My poor trousers seem destined for the laundry again. Second time today. Don't worry, Chloe.'

He stood up, looking down at Chloe, and her heart missed a beat. Even with soup-stained trousers he looked impossibly desirable. As he'd told her not to worry he'd automatically placed both hands on her upper arms. A frisson of sensual excitement ran through her but she knew she must remain calm and composed in front of the critical eyes of her family.

'It's time for bed, girls,' Chloe said quietly. 'You've both finished your soup so I'll take you upstairs now and read you a story.'

'Can Demetrius put us to bed and read us a story? Please, Mummy?' Rachel asked.

'Well, Demetrius is going to have his next course and—'

'I'd love to take the girls to their room,' Demetrius said. 'They're bathed and in their pyjamas so they'll only need to clean their teeth. And while they're doing that, I'll sponge some cold water on this spinach stain. Then we can have that story.'

'Don't stay too long, Demetrius,' Chloe said, before realising that everyone at the table was watching her.

It was as if she and Demetrius were already a family unit. They'd fallen into their roles so easily. But there were so many problems to overcome. She didn't yet know how Demetrius really felt about the way she'd deprived him of being a father for so long. Even if Demetrius could be persuaded to forgive her, how could she be sure that he wouldn't break her heart by turning her down as he had at the end of their affair? Demetrius might be enamoured by his daughters, but had his feelings towards their mother changed?

CHAPTER THREE

'CHLOE, I really think you ought to go upstairs and rescue Demetrius,' Pam said. 'You know what the twins are like when they don't want to go to bed. They're probably giving the poor man a hard time up there.'

'Oh, I'm sure Demetrius can handle two little girls, Mum,' Chloe said. 'He's a fully qualified, experienced doctor so he must have worked in paediatrics at some point. He'll come down when he's ready.'

'Yes, but Maria is waiting to serve the next course.'

'No, she's not,' Sara said quietly. 'When I went to the kitchen to speak to her, I suggested she and Manolis go home. I'll serve up when we're ready for the next course. Everything's on low heat in the oven so there's no hurry. Besides, we need to carry on with our wedding discussion, Mum. Do you really think we need six bridesmaids? I would prefer it if—'

'I think perhaps I will go up and check on the girls,' Chloe said quietly, as she pushed back her chair.

Somehow she was finding it difficult to concentrate on the arguments over bridesmaids and catering for the reception when there was a major crisis going on in her own life. As she went up the stairs to the girls' bedroom she could feel her heart beating with apprehension. Walking in through the open door of the pretty bedroom next door to her own, she paused to take in the touching scene. Samantha was sound asleep but next to her, sitting on the other bed, Demetrius was coming to the end of an obviously riveting story.

'And so they lived happily ever after.'

'Ah, that was so nice,' Rachel said. 'I like a happy end-ing, don't you, Demetrius?'

'I think everybody does.' Demetrius closed the book and stood up.

Rachel rubbed her eyes sleepily as she watched him. Chloe, standing in the doorway, knew that neither of them was aware that she had arrived. She remained absolutely still, unwilling to break the precious relationship that was developing between father and daughter.

Demetrius was smiling down at Rachel. 'Now, go to sleep, Rachel, and—'

'Aren't you going to kiss me goodnight, Demetrius?'

Demetrius bent down and kissed Rachel on the top of her head before straightening up. '*Kali nichte*, Rachel.'

Rachel turned her little face adoringly up towards Demetrius. 'That means goodnight, doesn't it? I know a lot of Greek now I go to school. My teacher says I speak Greek like the Greek children. *Kalinihta*, Demetrius.'

Chloe chose this moment to walk into the room. 'Good-night, Rachel,' she said, bending down to hug her daugh-ter.

Little arms encircled Chloe's neck as she kissed Rachel. Chloe loved these precious moments with her daughters at the end of the day. She couldn't bear to think what life would be without her little girls. They were a constant source of joy and happiness to her.

'Demetrius read me that story about the princess who married the handsome prince and they lived happily ever after. We live happily ever after, don't we, Mum?'

'We certainly do,' Chloe said softly, as she tucked the sheet around her daughter before turning her attention to Samantha.

It was a hot night, but Chloe felt it was safer to cover

the girls with a sheet in the summer. She'd plugged in the anti-mosquito appliance earlier in the evening but sometimes the odd intrepid mosquito managed to survive long enough to be a nuisance during the night.

Rachel had already closed her eyes and was falling into almost instant sleep. Chloe looked up at Demetrius. Silently, he took hold of her hand and led her out of the bedroom. On the landing he turned to face her. She could read nothing in the expression on his face but she knew it was an expression she would never forget. As long as she lived, she would remember this moment. The moment when she was forced to reveal the truth to the man she had always loved most in all the world.

'How could you?' Demetrius's eyes flashed with indignation.

'How could I…?'

'Chloe, the time for lies is finished.'

'I never lied to you! The situation was so impossible that—' As she was speaking she was aware that Demetrius's mobile was shrilling loudly in his pocket.

'You never lied because you didn't have to,' he said angrily, completely ignoring the shrilling phone. 'So long as you didn't contact me, that was OK as far as you were concerned. The fact that… I'd better answer this, it could be an emergency.'

He was reaching for his phone. 'Yes, Sister… I'm on my way.'

He cut the connection and his manner changed. It was as if they hadn't been in the middle of a poignant, life-changing experience.

'That was the hospital night superintendent. They need a doctor at the hospital. As I was the doctor who first examined the patient and ordered the treatment, Sister has asked if I'll go in. It's Fiona, our car crash victim.'

'She's on my ward. I'll come with you.'

'What about your family supper and the wedding plans?'

'Not important. They can sort out the wedding without me.'

Chloe sat quietly in the back of Michaelis's car as he drove her and Demetrius back to the hospital. Demetrius, sitting in the front passenger seat, kept up a constant flow of conversation with Michaelis, asking questions about hospital procedure and the setting up of the operating theatre if he needed to perform surgery during the night.

Chloe listened but didn't join in the conversation. She could have answered Demetrius's questions herself but felt it would be more reassuring for him to hear the answers from the hospital medical director.

'I'm really grateful that you've taken up the reins so quickly, Demetrius,' Michaelis said, as he swung the car into the hospital forecourt. 'You're just the sort of doctor we need. It makes my job as medical director so much easier when all the staff pull their weight.'

Michaelis turned off the engine and reached inside the glove compartment. 'Here are the keys to the hospital car, Demetrius. We keep a spare car for new doctors who haven't yet got their own transport. Use it until you've got your own wheels.'

'Thanks, Michaelis. I'm going to look at a four-wheel-drive tomorrow, actually.'

'Now, you're sure you don't want me to come into hospital with you and give you some help?'

'Absolutely not!' Demetrius said, alighting from the passenger seat and holding open the back door for Chloe. 'Chloe and I will be able to cope, with the help of the night staff. Besides, you ought to get back to the discussions about your wedding.'

Michaelis groaned. 'Don't remind me! Sara and I are so happy living in my house. If I had my way, we'd go away to one of the tiny churches at the other side of the island and come back married. Now, if there's a medical problem you can't handle, ring my mobile.'

Demetrius closed the car door. '*Kalinihta*, Michaelis.'

Chloe went into the cloakroom and quickly changed into her uniform. Demetrius had already gone up to the ward. Hurrying along the deserted corridor, Chloe was aware of the different ambience that enveloped the hospital during the night. Everything was quiet except for the occasional muted sound of a telephone, the hacking sound of a persistent cough or the feeble cry from an old person or child who needed reassurance that there was someone to help them during the long dark hours before the dawn.

Demetrius was bending over their patient. Sister Irini, the night superintendent, who was beside him turned to greet Chloe.

'Thanks for coming, Chloe. I wouldn't have called for help if I hadn't been so busy on the other wards. Fiona was so distraught. She asked specifically for Dr Demetrius because she said he would know what to do. And, according to the notes, you performed the ultrasound scan, didn't you, Chloe?'

'Yes. Now, what's the problem, Irini?'

Demetrius straightened up from his examination of the patient. 'You can leave Chloe in charge here, Irini. We'll handle this.'

'Thanks, Demetrius. You can call me if you need my help.'

The small, navy blue clad sister hurried away to attend

to her other duties. Demetrius took Chloe to one side and quietly filled her in on the situation that had arisen.

'Fiona has started bleeding. She's also experiencing considerable abdominal pain. I've examined her and the uterus feels hard, like wood, to the touch.'

'And the foetal heartbeat?' Chloe asked anxiously.

'Still there, but not so strong as it was.'

'Are you thinking what I'm thinking, Demetrius?'

For an instant, a hint of irritation crossed Demetrius's handsome but now strained-looking face. 'I'm not psychic, Chloe. Tell me what you're thinking.'

She lowered her voice. 'Placental abruption?'

Demetrius nodded. 'We'll need another ultrasound scan to confirm our diagnosis, but I think we'll find there's been a complete or partial separation of the placenta from the uterus.'

'We'll take Fiona next door now and do the scan. The placenta was in place when we checked this morning,' Chloe said.

'But the wrenching movements Fiona made when the car crashed must have weakened it, so that now it's become dislodged. We need to know just how badly the placenta has been injured, Chloe. After the scan we can assess the situation. I'm going to take blood for grouping and cross-matching. The bleeding has eased off but I may need to give Fiona a transfusion. And we need to check on her kidney function to see if there's been some damage there.'

'I tested Fiona's urine sample earlier, Demetrius. It was clear of protein so I think we can rule out kidney damage.'

Demetrius nodded. 'Good.'

They returned to the patient. Demetrius explained that they needed another ultrasound.

'I'm not going to lose Tommy, am I, Sister?' Fiona

asked as, clinging to Chloe's hand, she was wheeled through into the scanning room.

'We're doing everything we can, Fiona,' Chloe said gently. 'Let's see what the scan shows. Tommy's heart is still beating steadily, so there's a good chance he's going to survive.'

'Yes, but he's gone very quiet.' Fiona gave a little sob. 'He's not happy. I can tell he's having a hard time in there. Couldn't you just get him out now and put him in an incubator?'

'We could certainly do that, Fiona,' Demetrius said, patiently. 'But at thirty weeks, little Tommy would have to struggle to survive in the outside world. He needs to be tucked up in your womb for as long as we can keep him there.'

They had eased the patient onto the ultrasound scanning table and Chloe was spreading the special cream over the distended abdomen. She could feel the hardness of the uterus and deduced there was some concealed bleeding inside there.

'I'll get the nursing staff to keep a check on the girth of the abdomen, Demetrius,' she told him quietly.

Demetrius nodded as he switched on the ultrasound machine. 'So long as it doesn't increase any more, there's a good chance the placenta isn't harmed too much... Yes, there it is...'

He pointed to the whirling images on the screen. 'Since this morning, there's been a partial separation just here.'

'What's happening?' Fiona tried to raise herself on her elbows so that she could see the screen more easily.

Demetrius patted her hand. 'The placenta has pulled away slightly from the wall of the uterus. That's what's causing the bleeding you've experienced. The tear is very small but we need to ensure it doesn't get any bigger.

You'll need to rest completely for the next few weeks if we're to keep up the supply of nourishment to your baby.'

Fiona stared at Demetrius. 'But I'm flying back to England in ten days. Dave has to go back to work.'

'You *were* flying back in ten days,' Demetrius said solemnly. 'If you want to save your baby's life you'll have to stay here.'

Chloe took hold of her patient's hand. 'Don't worry, Fiona. We'll sort everything out when your husband comes in. We'll make sure he knows you'll be in good hands now that he'll have to leave you behind. Would you like me to call him now so that he can be with you through the night?'

Fiona nodded mutely. 'I'll give you his number.'

Back in the ward, after phoning Fiona's husband, Chloe instructed the night staff about the treatment required for their patient. Fiona needed round-the-clock checking of temperature, pulse and blood pressure, besides twice daily measuring of the girth of the abdomen and checks for protein in the urine.

'But the most important part of the treatment is that Fiona should remain at rest in her bed,' Chloe concluded, turning to smile reassuringly at her patient.

Fiona gave a wry grimace. 'For how long?'

'You're thirty weeks pregnant now. In patients with your condition we usually try to hold off delivery until thirty-eight weeks.'

'Heavens, I'll have to take up knitting!'

Fiona smiled. 'Not if you don't want to, but I'll send along the occupational therapist in the morning. She's always full of ideas for keeping patients from getting bored.'

Fiona groaned. 'I wish I'd stayed at home instead of coming out here.'

Chloe patted her patient's hand. 'It's tough on you, I

know, Fiona. But it will be worth it if we can save your baby.'

'If…did you say *if*?' Fiona looked from Chloe to Demetrius.

Demetrius nodded gravely. 'There's still an element of doubt, Fiona. You've got to take your treatment seriously or—'

'I will, Doctor! I'll really try to be patient. It's just that…it's my first baby and…everything seemed so strange anyway, but now it's even worse.'

Chloe sat down on the bed and put her arms around the sobbing young woman.

'Having a first baby is never easy, Fiona,' Chloe said. 'I remember being so scared when I had my twins that—'

'Twins! You've got twins, Sister?'

The sobbing had ceased as Fiona pulled herself up against her pillows. 'How old are they?'

Chloe glanced up at Demetrius who was watching her with an enigmatic expression. 'Seven…nearly eight.'

'And did you have any more babies after that?'

Chloe shook her head. 'No, I'm a widow now.'

'Oh, you poor thing! That's why you're having to work, is it?'

'I like working and I love nursing. Wouldn't change my job for anything.' Chloe stood up, very much aware that Demetrius's eyes were on her.

'I'll see you in the morning, Fiona,' Demetrius said, moving away from the bedside. 'Are you leaving now, Chloe?'

Chloe turned away from her patient to look at Demetrius. His expression had changed from the caring, professional doctor mode he'd adopted when they'd worked together. He was once more her erstwhile lover, avid for more information about why he'd been left in the dark for so long. She would have liked to have stayed on in the limbo land of the hospital but knew that she couldn't postpone their confrontation any longer.

'Yes, I'm coming, Demetrius,' she said. 'Goodnight, Fiona.'

As Demetrius drove the car along the shore of Nimborio Bay, Chloe looked out over the water through the open passenger window. Neither of them had spoken to each other since leaving the hospital.

'Would you please pull in at the side of the road, Demetrius?' Chloe asked. 'We need to talk and we won't be able to do that when we get back to my house. I hadn't realised how late it was. It's after midnight so everybody will be in bed.'

Demetrius manoeuvred the car into a tiny space at the side of the narrow road. Below them, the side of the valley dropped steeply into the dark, mysterious depths of the sea.

'What you mean is that if we start having a row, we'll waken everybody,' Demetrius said wryly.

'Exactly!' Chloe opened the passenger door and scrambled out.

She needed air, she needed to escape the claustrophobic atmosphere of the car. She needed time to assess the situation she found herself in. Here she was in this idyllic spot above the water with the man she could have loved unconditionally for ever and ever—if only he'd wanted her to stay with him.

She caught her breath as the memories came flooding back. Her feet, as if drawn by some unseen magnetic force, moved towards the narrow goat track that led down to the water's edge. Carefully, she made her way over the rough stones, revelling in the feeling of freedom, the scent of the herbs on the side of the hill and above all the quiet, the utter silence of the night disturbed only by the occasional rustling of the leaves in the trees or the plaintive cry of a sleepless lamb.

'Where are you going, Chloe?'

Demetrius, breathless from hurrying to catch up with her, materialised in the moonlit darkness by the side of the water. Chloe sank down on a large rock. It was still warm from the heat of the day, but cooling rapidly. She ran her fingers over its timeless surface, wishing she could turn back the clock and start again with Demetrius. Wipe the slate clean and go back to the days when they had been so young and carefree.

'I think I was running away,' she said quietly.

'Running away? From me?'

Unbidden, the tears began to trickle down her cheeks. 'Oh, Demetrius, if only…'

He knelt down beside the rock and drew her into his arms. 'Chloe, don't cry, my darling. I didn't mean to upset you. It's all been such a shock for me. I had no idea…'

He was dabbing at her eyes with a large white handkerchief. Gently, he pulled her to her feet and stood looking down at her, still holding her gently in his arms. In the moonlight she could see the solemn expression on his ruggedly handsome face.

'Now, don't you think you owe me an explanation?' he asked. 'Tell me what happened after you left the island. September, wasn't it?'

She drew in her breath. 'Yes, it was the middle of September, eight years ago at the end of the summer.'

'So tell me the medical details of your pregnancy,' he said, in a matter-of-fact, professional-style voice, as if Chloe's pregnancy had been the most natural outcome of that idyllic summer together.

'Yes, Doctor,' she said solemnly, raising her eyes to his.

He smiled and she felt herself relaxing. 'I'm trying to be objective, Chloe. If you just give me the details as if it were a medical report…'

'But it's not a medical report. It's about you and me!' She kicked at a pebble in the sand with her foot. 'I'll try to be objective if I can, but you've got to understand it's a very emotive subject for me.'

'I understand.' He bent his head and kissed her gently on the lips. 'I shouldn't have done that but I've wanted to kiss you for hours.'

She raised her head in surprise. 'Have you? But I thought you were angry with me.'

'Only because you'd kept this big, important secret from me. I still…' Demetrius checked himself from saying too much. Chloe had made it perfectly clear she hadn't wanted him when she'd left the island after their affair.

Chloe took a deep breath before she began her explanation. 'When I went back to England, I planned to tell Patrick that I'd decided we should end our relationship. We'd both agreed to have three months apart to sort out our feelings for each other. I was going to be on Ceres with my parents, Patrick was going to go backpacking in Thailand. We'd also agreed that we wouldn't contact each other during that three months so that we could make a true assessment of the situation.'

Demetrius raised one eyebrow. 'It sounds very formal.'

'The arrangement had to be formal,' Chloe said quietly. 'A true assessment of the situation. Those were Patrick's words, not mine. But he knew as well as I did that we'd both been coasting along for some time together. We'd got used to each other, we'd always been there for each other since we were small. It was a stale relationship that needed shaking up or ending.'

'And you'd decided to end it.'

'Quite definitely. I'd thought it through during the first couple of weeks I was out here and I knew Patrick and I couldn't go on as we had been doing. I'd decided to end it as soon as I got back. And then I met you…and that finally convinced me that I only loved Patrick as a brother. I was all fired up to tell him at the end of the three months' separation we'd agreed on. He was upset but we'd been friends since childhood and we knew we'd stay that way. And then…' She paused, searching for the right way to explain the next bit of her revelation. 'My period was two weeks late.'

'So you told Patrick.'

Chloe took a deep breath. 'I'd told him about you, our affair, everything. Emotionally I was a mess, and he helped me. Then he came up with the idea of getting married.'

'What did he say?'

Chloe ran a hand through her hair distractedly. 'Patrick insisted it was the right thing to do. We both knew where we stood and we'd do it for the baby's sake.'

Chloe picked up a pebble, turning it in her hands as the memories of that evening with Patrick flooded back.

'He wanted to bring up the baby as his own—we didn't, of course, know I was carrying twins at that point. So we announced a brief engagement and our families were delighted. Discovering that I was carrying twins convinced me I was doing the right thing.'

Demetrius pulled her towards him in a protective gesture.

She snuggled against him. 'I never experienced real love until I met you…'

'Say it, Chloe. Please, tell me that you were in love with me.'

'I think it was love at first sight, if there is such a thing,' she said softly, relieved at last to be able to talk freely about the time when she'd been truly happy. 'I remember it was a couple of weeks or so after I'd arrived on Ceres. I'd been across to Rhodes for the day to do some shopping. And as I'd trawled around the shops looking for summer clothes, I'd finally come to the conclusion that I had to end the relationship with Patrick. All the way back to Ceres I knew I'd made the right decision at last. The ferry arrived in Ceres harbour and I was walking onto the quay-side.'

'I remember,' Demetrius said. 'I remember looking across at the ferry, standing up, moving forward so I could be near you when you got off the ferry. You were wearing a white jersey because it was windy that evening. I'd seen you before down at the harbour but I'd never had the nerve to walk up and say, "Hello, I'm Demetrius, can I buy you a drink?"'

Chloe smiled. 'Do you remember when you took hold of my hand to help me off the ferry?'

Her words were coming out in a tremendous rush as she remembered the magical touch of Demetrius's fingers as this handsome stranger had reached forward from the quayside.

'I'd never seen you before in my life,' she continued, breathless with remembered excitement. 'But you came out from among the crowd of people who were meeting friends off the boat and simply took me away with you to sit outside that taverna, the one with the wobbly chairs and the parrot in the cage that kept shrieking if the music stopped.'

'I remember,' Demetrius said, his voice husky.

'You asked me if I wanted a drink and then we sat looking at each other, talking endlessly, finding out every-thing we could about each other.'

He leaned forward now, putting his hands on either side

of her face as he kissed her once more. This time his kiss deepened. She suppressed the ecstatic sigh that threatened to escape her lips. All her anguished thoughts were vanishing. She only knew that she was here on a deserted shore in the middle of the night with the man she knew she was destined to love all her life. Whether he returned that love didn't matter any more so long as she could be with him.

Demetrius could feel Chloe responding to his caresses. He, too, had abandoned all thoughts of remaining cool and objective. His precious Chloe was here in his arms and more than anything else in the world he wanted to make love to her. He wanted to reclaim what was his. This lovely body, with its perfect contours…

He ran his fingers gently over the smooth skin covering her spine. She was arching her back, revelling in his caresses. He dared to unhook her bra and she moaned in anticipation as his fingers gently teased her breasts. He could feel himself hardening and knew that he was reaching the point of no return. The strong desires urging him on were demanding fulfilment.

He ought to hold off. If Chloe tried to put an end to their love-making now, he would make a valiant effort to tear himself away from her.

But Chloe was breathing heavily, unable to control her response to the wildly romantic, sensual stimulation of Demetrius's caresses. She felt young again, completely abandoned. It was as if the last eight years had never happened. Tonight she'd met Demetrius for the first time. Yes, it had been love at first sight and she knew that this was the only man in the world for her…

Chloe awoke to the sound of the sea lapping on the shores of the bay. Her head was resting on a rolled-up piece of cloth. Looking more closely, she saw that it was Demetrius's orange shirt. She sat up quickly. In the pre-dawn light, she could just make out his solitary figure down by the water's edge. He was picking up a pebble, skimming it across the water as she'd seen him do so many times during the idyllic time they'd shared so long ago.

Her body felt so good! Her skin still tingled with the aftermath of their love-making. As they'd made love, clinging to each other, the sandy shore had seemed as wonderful as a feather bed. She remembered everything now, Demetrius putting his shirt under her head as she'd drifted off into a blissful sleep. She looked up at the sky, feeling that she should send up a prayer of thanksgiving to whichever god had seen fit to return her Greek hero to her.

Maybe it was one of the gods on Mount Olympus and she'd been turned into a Greek goddess! She smiled as the confused, childish thoughts ran through her mind. When she'd been very young, she'd been fascinated by the stories of Greek mythology. She'd never thought she would wake up on a Greek island shore with her own Greek hero.

A cloud was drifting across the moon and she shivered. Her Greek hero was here with her now, but for how long? And what about the twins? She hadn't explained to Demetrius why she'd had to keep them secret from him all these years. In the cold light of day, there were going to have to be more explanations. Making love with Demetrius had been out of this world, but she had to come back to earth now and face her problems again.

Demetrius turned and saw she was awake. He came over the shore towards her, holding out his hand to help her to her feet. She picked up the shirt.

'You ought to put this on, Demetrius. It's chilly down here by the water.'

'I hadn't noticed.'

He was standing looking down at her with a sad expression on his face. Chloe knew that the cares of the world were crowding in on Demetrius again. They'd shared a brief idyll and now they had to shoulder their responsibilities.

She looked up at him, her eyes pleading for co-operation. 'Demetrius, I want to explain why I couldn't let you know about the twins. Before the twins were born, Patrick made me promise not to reveal that he wasn't their father. He wanted everyone to think they were his so that neither his family nor mine was upset.'

Demetrius frowned. 'Would it upset your family to know that I'm the twins' father?'

She hesitated before speaking. 'I need to prepare the ground. All these years…'

'And how will Patrick's parents react if they find out he wasn't the twins' father?'

'I didn't tell you, did I?' She hesitated as the sad memory of that awful day came back to her. 'Patrick's parents died with him in the crash.'

'How terrible for you! I…I'm sorry. I don't know what to say.'

For a few moments, Demetrius was quiet, seemingly lost in his own thoughts. When he spoke, his voice was husky with emotion.

'Chloe, I'm sorry you've suffered all these family problems, but it doesn't change the fact that Rachel and Samantha are my own flesh and blood. I need to be a part of their life. You've kept them from me long enough, so the sooner you accept that…'

'Please, Demetrius. Just give me time to work out what I'm going to tell my parents. I know that in spite of the fact we've just made love, nothing's changed between us.

You made it clear that you didn't want a permanent relationship with me before, and—'

'I made it clear? What are you talking about?'

Demetrius stared down at Chloe, baffled by what she'd just said. He was searching his mind for a clue as to what he might have said to her that had given her the impression he hadn't wanted her. He remembered only too well that last evening when he'd waited for her and she hadn't turned up. That had signified that she was leaving him to go back to Patrick and that other life in which he could play no part.

'It doesn't matter now,' Chloe said quickly. 'I don't want this to develop into a full-scale row. It's all in the past and we have to pick up the pieces and move on. If you will only be patient, I promise I'll acknowledge you as the girls' father.'

'When?'

'In a few weeks.'

'A few weeks! Meanwhile, I'm supposed to continue living a lie, seeing the girls and letting them think I'm just a good friend of the family?'

'Perhaps it would be better if you didn't see the girls until—'

'Oh, no! They're my daughters. I love them already and I think they're very fond of me. You've deprived me of my rightful fatherhood for long enough. Now it's my turn to state the rules.'

Looking up at Demetrius, Chloe couldn't believe this was the same wonderful, caring, considerate man who'd driven her wild with his passionate love-making during the night. He was still infinitely desirable. If he were to take her in his arms now, she would be in danger of giving herself again and again until, sated once more with ecstatic fulfilment she would find it difficult not to comply with any demands he made about their daughters.

But she was standing well back from him until she had her treacherous body under control. Her body mustn't have any influence over her mind. And she knew she had to insist that they take their time over their explanation to the family.

'Sara and Michaelis are going to be married in August,' Chloe said evenly. 'My parents are working very hard towards making the event a success. Nobody talks about anything else but the wedding at home. If I were to confess that you were the father of their granddaughters at this moment... Please, Demetrius, let's leave the announcement until after the wedding.'

Demetrius looked down at Chloe. He could see how distressed she was. This wonderful girl who'd lain in his arms during the night, just as she had in that distant time when he'd thought she would always be with him. Two hours ago he'd been the happiest man in the world, but as this incredible night ended he knew that nothing had changed.

Chloe had left him for another man before. He couldn't believe it at the time. Couldn't believe that she could have loved him with such intensity for three months and then simply walked away. Making love with Chloe was totally separate from spending a lifetime together. He still loved her but he knew she would never commit herself to him entirely.

So, because he loved her, he couldn't hurt her by going against her wishes where the twins were concerned. He didn't want to cause her any more unhappiness. He raised his eyes to the thin band of red sky hovering over the hill across the bay, heralding the approaching dawn.

'A new day, a new beginning,' he said quietly, almost

to himself. 'Yesterday I had no idea I was a father. Today I should be celebrating the wonderful miracle that happened without me knowing it. Two daughters!'

He looked down at Chloe and touched her cheek. 'Thank you for giving birth to my daughters,' he said, his voice husky with emotion. 'I'll try to keep the secret until after your sister's wedding, but I can't guarantee your family won't guess the truth during the next few weeks. The twins are my own flesh and blood and I'm only human.'

CHAPTER FOUR

'THE baby's head's crowning, Sister,' Demetrius told Chloe.

Although Demetrius's tone was measured, Chloe detected the sense of urgency in his manner. Over the past ten days, she'd worked side by side with him on many occasions and they'd established a good professional working relationship. The fact that their personal life was in turmoil didn't seem to affect their hospital work in any way. They were both experienced, well-trained professionals and, whatever had happened between them, the patient always came first.

Chloe took hold of their patient's hand. 'We'd like you to start panting again, Nicoletta…yes, get the rhythm going like I showed you… Keep going…'

Chloe found herself panting alongside the patient, willing her not to push down at this crucial time in the birth. Demetrius had said he could see the baby's head crowning at the top of the birth passage. This meant that Nicoletta was fully dilated and the baby's head would ease itself out slowly. The essential thing was that the head wasn't thrust out too quickly by the mother forcing the pace.

'Good. Well done, Nicoletta,' Demetrius said, holding the emerging head to control the speed of its exit. 'You can relax for a moment. Would you like to see baby's head?'

They didn't suggest this to every patient, but Chloe knew that Demetrius would have noticed what a sensible, intelligent girl Nicoletta was. Ever since the young Greek mother-to-be had arrived at the hospital earlier that morning they had both been impressed by her calm control and co-operation. It was her first baby but the young mother was a natural. Both Demetrius and Chloe herself were speaking in Greek to their patient—Demetrius rather more fluently than she did! But she was coping much better than she had when she'd first started working at the hospital, and there was a good relaxed atmosphere here in the delivery suite.

'Oh, I'd love to see my baby's head!'

Nicoletta was struggling to raise herself on her elbows. Chloe put an arm around the patient's back to support her as she gazed down at the miracle of the baby's head emerging from her body.

'Oh, look at that beautiful little head!' Nicoletta exclaimed in a breathless, excited voice. 'See the dark hair all wet and messed up, but it still looks lovely, doesn't it? *Horaya, horaya*, beautiful, beautiful!'

Chloe wiped a piece of gauze over Nicoletta's eyes. Their patient was crying with happiness and relief that her baby was nearly there, and the tears were making it impossible to see clearly.

Nicoletta sank back on her pillows as Demetrius slid a finger under her pubic arch to check the whereabouts of the umbilical cord. Chloe, watching, saw Demetrius was satisfied that it wasn't around the baby's neck. The birth could proceed.

The next contraction completed the delivery. Demetrius brought the baby out and placed it on their patient's abdomen. The cord was cut and the now squalling infant handed to his mother.

'A boy! We both wanted a boy.' Nicoletta was weeping with joy again, unwrapping the dressing towel from her baby to check him over. 'He's got ten little fingers and ten little toes! He's perfect. We're going to call him Vasilio after my father.'

Chloe looked across the patient at Demetrius. Even though they'd both delivered countless babies during the course of their professional careers they were always deeply moved at the sight of a young mother with her first child. Chloe could see her own excitement mirrored in Demetrius's eyes but there was something else. A deep underlying sadness.

Would he ever be able to forgive her for withholding his own babies from him? Perhaps when she agreed to reveal that he was the twins' father the healing process might start. Seeing the sad expression in Demetrius's eyes, she wondered if he was thinking about the birth of the twins, wishing he'd been there to hold them in his arms as soon as they'd been born.

Since that wonderful night by the sea she'd been on tenterhooks, wondering whether Demetrius would jump the gun. But, like the honourable man he was, he'd remained silent. But today, the twins' birthday, it was crucial that he shouldn't take it upon himself to arrive at the house. For the past few days, she'd deliberately avoided all personal contact with him during her off-duty times, hurrying back home as soon as she was free.

In professional mode now, Chloe went through the post-natal checks before settling mother and baby in the ward. Demetrius was called away to another patient. She had only to work until lunchtime today and then, having taken a half-day off duty, she could hurry back to finish organising the birthday party.

Chloe bent over her patient, combing back the dark hair that was still damp with the perspiration of her exertions.

'Your hair will need washing, Nicoletta,' Chloe said.

'Perhaps it will be better to leave it for a day or two until you get home.'

She put the comb down on the locker and smiled down at her patient. 'You're in very good shape again so there's no reason why you shouldn't go home tomorrow if you feel strong enough to cope.'

Nicoletta hesitated. 'Well, there's a bit of a problem. We're living with my husband's mother. She's rather bossy and I don't feel I can face her for a few days. She thinks she's an expert on everything—especially babies— and because I'm only nineteen and we've only been married three months—that was a bit of a shock for her, I can tell you! What I'm trying to say is, could I stay in for two or three days till I get to know which end of my baby is which? I'd like to go home as a mum with some experience rather than as a complete novice.'

'Of course you can, Nicoletta! We've got some spare beds at the moment so unless we get several emergency deliveries at once you could stay for a few days until you feel strong enough to cope with life in the outside world. We like our new mothers to be happy when they leave us.'

'Fantastic! You've been so kind to me, both you and the doctor.'

Chloe smiled. 'You're a good patient. A natural mother, I would say. Would you like me to put Vasilio in the nursery for a while so you can get some rest?'

'No, thanks. I'd like to keep him here with me, just in case he gets hungry again. And Costas, my husband, is going to come in soon. His ship is due to dock in the harbour this morning—he works on the inter-island fer-ries—and he'll come straight here to meet his son.'

Chloe could feel a lump in her throat as she watched the young mother cuddling her baby against her breast.

She remembered how she'd felt when the twins were born and how her own happiness had been overshadowed by the fact that she hadn't been able to share her joy with their real father.

She remembered the expression in Demetrius's eyes when he'd looked at her soon after they'd delivered Nicoletta's baby. There had been so much pain hidden behind his tender expression. He must have been wondering what it had been like when their daughters had been born. Had he been wishing he'd been there to hold them in his arms soon after they'd arrived in the world?

She gave herself a mental shake and, as she always did when she started down that hypothetical road, told herself that it was impossible to change the past. She'd survived the difficult times so far. The unknown future lay ahead of her and it was how she handled her delicate relationship with Demetrius that was now the most important thing in her life.

She still loved Demetrius, of that she'd never had any doubt. But when she'd lain in his arms by the shore only days ago, she'd known it had only been a brief escape from the normal pattern of her life. She must try not to become too emotionally involved, because Demetrius couldn't change.

During the three months they'd been together during that life-changing summer, she'd been convinced that they would stay together for ever. But in the final days before she'd been due to go back to England, she'd known she would have to tell Patrick that their relationship was over and, which had been equally daunting, she would have to tell her parents what was happening.

She'd kept her relationship with Demetrius secret deliberately, feeling that Patrick should be the first one to be informed about her decision to stay on Ceres. But as the time had approached when she'd have to bring everything out into the open, she'd begun to get cold feet about the big step she was taking. She began to wonder if she was doing the right thing.

What had Patrick decided? You couldn't have a long relationship with someone without worrying when you wanted to end it. Would he be devastated by her decision? She remembered that Demetrius had sensed her unease and she'd confessed to having second thoughts. She'd told Demetrius she loved him; she'd said her doubts were only temporary. Patrick had been part of her life for so long that it was going to be a tremendous change. Demetrius had told her she must be absolutely sure this was what she wanted.

And then, all of a sudden, Demetrius had made the decision for her. When he'd sent her that heart-breaking letter, saying it was over between them, she'd known she had to return to England.

She turned as she heard footsteps coming down the ward. Demetrius had changed out of theatre greens into casual trousers and an open-necked shirt. He looked cool and calm as he approached Nicoletta's bed.

'How're you feeling now, Nicoletta?'

Chloe watched Demetrius leaning over their patient, checking that she was comfortable and unworried about her stay in hospital.

'I'll have to leave you,' Chloe said quietly. 'Kate is taking charge of the ward this afternoon. I've got a half-day off.'

'Wait a moment, Chloe,' Demetrius said evenly. He smiled down at his patient. 'I'll see you again tomorrow, Nicoletta.'

Chloe waited for Demetrius to walk down the ward with

her. She handed over the keys to Kate before going into her office, and Demetrius followed her.

'I've got a half-day off as well,' Demetrius said quietly, pushing the door closed behind him.

'I thought you looked in a relaxed mood,' Chloe said, removing her cap and shaking out her hair. 'What did you want to see me about?'

'I've been invited to the twins' birthday party.'

Chloe stared at him. When she'd partially recovered from the shock she found her voice.

'I think you must be mistaken, Demetrius. I gave out all the invitations and, I'm sorry, but you weren't on the list.'

'Anthony invited me.'

'My father? No! He couldn't have. Why would he…?'

Her awful suspicions were beginning to make sense. The strange looks her father had often given her. The way he always went to great lengths to explain why the twins had dark hair whilst her own was blonde and Patrick's not much darker. How long had her father known?

She sank down into the nearest chair. 'When did Dad invite you, Demetrius?'

'He phoned me at the hospital a couple of days ago.'

'But did he say why he was inviting you? I mean, it's a children's tea party, with just a few mums and dads coming along because…' Her voice trailed away as she watched the slow smile spreading across Demetrius's face.

'Exactly!' he said softly, his voice husky with emotion. 'That's why I'm invited. A few mums and dads, you said. Well, I'm the most important dad of them all so don't you think—?'

'Demetrius, you promised! You said you would wait until after Sara's wedding in August. You said you would give me time to think out a solution to the problem.'

He raised one eyebrow. 'Just like I gave you time to decide if you were going to stay on Ceres or go back to England?'

'That's not the same! You're twisting my words. Did my father say why he was inviting you?'

Demetrius reached out and drew her towards him. As his muscular arms encircled her, she tried to hold back.

'Demetrius, holding me close isn't going to solve anything. We both know that we get carried away when we're near to each other. But it doesn't solve anything…it doesn't make it any easier…'

She gazed up into his eyes, helpless against the power of her treacherous body and her turbulent emotions. This was the first time Demetrius had held her like this since leaving the shore where they'd made love. She'd been so careful to keep control of her emotions, but now Demetrius's wickedly irresistible charm was melting down all her defences.

Gently, he lowered his head and placed his lips against hers. She gave an involuntary sigh as the touch of his lips removed the last shred of her resolution. But even as she felt her body melting, moulding itself against his, she somehow found the strength of will to pull herself away.

'No, Demetrius. You're only trying to get round me, hoping that I'll accept the idea that you're coming to the house this afternoon. We agreed…'

He placed one hand gently over her lips. 'Shh. Don't go upsetting yourself. There's something I have to tell you about your father. I think he's guessed the truth about the twins. He suspects I'm their father.'

Chloe drew in her breath. 'If that's true, in a way, I'm almost relieved. It's been such a strain, wondering if he knew. The things he said, the way he behaved sometimes… It all made me wonder if he was more intuitive than everybody else.'

Demetrius dropped his arms to his sides and walked over to the window, looking down into the busy harbourside. 'Yes, your father is exceptionally intuitive, but he had a head start on the others. You see, he knew that you and I had been lovers.'

He turned back to look at Chloe as he heard her gasp of astonishment.

'But how could he possibly know that? We were so careful. My family never saw us together. You never came to the house or—'

'I did come to the house,' Demetrius said quietly. 'One time when you weren't there. I went to see your father.'

'No! He never told me. When was that?'

'When I sensed that you were having second thoughts about remaining on Ceres. You said everyone expected you to go home to England and get engaged to your childhood sweetheart and you would soon have to tell everyone of your change of heart. I phoned your father and asked if I could come and see him on a private matter when the rest of the family wouldn't be there. We arranged a convenient time. I believe you were shopping in the town with your mother. Your elder sister, Francesca, had only spent a week on Ceres before going back to England and Sara was in France.'

Demetrius paused to watch Chloe's reaction to the unfolding revelation. She was looking apprehensive.

'So what did you say to my father?'

'I told him that I was in love with you and I wanted to marry you. Your father asked if you felt the same way as I did. I said I couldn't be sure but you'd given me every reason to hope that you did.'

'Oh, Demetrius!' Chloe turned away as she saw the look of anguish in his eyes. 'And how did my father respond?'

'Your father said there were plans ahead for you to become engaged to Patrick, that the two of you had seemed destined to marry ever since you were small. I then pointed out that you'd decided to end your relationship with Patrick before I started seeing you. I explained that you and Patrick had deliberately split up for three months so that you could sort out your feelings for each other.'

Chloe drew in her breath. 'And what did Dad say?'

'He said he'd noticed that the two of you hadn't appeared to be getting on with each other for a while but he thought it was just a phase you were going through.'

Demetrius leaned forward as if to emphasise a point. 'I said it wasn't a phase. It was a definite split. I asked your father if he would give me his permission to marry you if you agreed. He remained quiet for a few moments, I remember, and then he said that your happiness was his primary concern. If that was what you wanted then he would gladly give his blessing to our marriage. But he said it was a big step to make and he hoped you would make the right decision. He also said he didn't want your mother to hear about the possibility of a change of plan until all decisions had been made.'

'Chloe!' The door burst open and Kate came in. 'Thank goodness you're still here... Oh, sorry Demetrius, I didn't know you were here.'

'That's OK, Kate, I was just going.'

Demetrius was making for the door.

'Demetrius!' Chloe called.

There was a wry, mischievous smile on his face as he turned in the doorway. 'See you later, Chloe!'

'Sorry, Chloe,' Katerina said. 'I hope I didn't come at a bad time.'

Chloe gave a sigh of exasperation as she realised that she mustn't take out her frustration on her staff nurse.

'Couldn't have been worse, but you weren't to know that.' Chloe took a deep breath to calm herself and move back into professional mode. 'Now, what can I do for you before I go off duty, Kate?'

The problem was quickly sorted. In answer to Kate's query, Chloe explained that the new drug she'd ordered for one of the patients hadn't arrived yet, which was why it couldn't be found on the medicine trolley.

'The dispensary assure me they can deliver it this afternoon. Sorry, Kate, I should have told you. I've got so many things on my mind today.'

'It's the twins' birthday party, isn't it? It must be hard work, organising all those games for a crowd of kids.'

Chloe raised her eyebrows. 'That's the least of my worries!' She gathered up her things. 'See you tomorrow, Kate.'

'Enjoy yourself!'

As she went out of her office Chloe reflected that all she wanted to do was to survive the afternoon without too many secrets coming out.

'Demetrius! You came!' Rachel ran across the terrace towards him, her little arms outstretched in rapturous welcome. 'Samantha and I asked Mummy if you were coming but she said you would be too busy at the hospital.'

'Well, I'm here now. I made a special effort to get a half-day off duty,' Demetrius said, kneeling down so that he could return the little girl's hug.

Samantha, hanging behind her sister, then came shyly forward and gave Demetrius a kiss on the cheek.

Chloe, talking to a couple of mothers, watched the touching spectacle out of the corner of her eye. Seeing how

much the girls already liked Demetrius, it made her feel
even worse about depriving them for so long. And she felt
guilty that she'd insisted on excluding Demetrius from
their birthday party.

Quietly, she excused herself from the small group of
adults and went over to the edge of the terrace. She needed
time to think of a strategy as to how to behave towards
Demetrius during the party. He was here now and there
was nothing she could do about that. It was how she reacted to him that would matter.

Her father had been away for a couple of days at the
hospital on Rhodes. He'd been asked to give a lecture to
the medical students there. Although he always maintained
that he was retired, Chloe knew it was good for his self-
esteem whenever he was requested to use his professional
experience. So occasionally he agreed to put on a suit and
go over the water. Anthony had promised to get back as
soon as he could to be with his darling granddaughters on
their birthday.

Chloe was still reeling from the revelation that
Demetrius had actually discussed their situation with
Anthony all those years ago. No wonder her father had put
two and two together when the twins were born. No one
else had questioned the supposition that her tiny twin
babies had been born after an eight-month pregnancy.
Twins were often early.

She could hear Rachel and Samantha shouting with excitement as they unwrapped the large parcels that
Demetrius had brought for them.

'Snorkels and flippers!' Rachel exclaimed in delight.
'Mine are pink—what colour are yours, Samantha? Get the
paper off quickly. Blue—lovely, your favourite colour!
Wow! We've been asking Mum for ages if we could have
some but she said we had to wait until we were a bit older.'

'Well, today you're eight, not seven like you were yesterday,' Demetrius said. 'So I thought you would be old enough to have some lessons in snorkelling.'

'Will you teach us, Demetrius?'

Chloe moved back across the terrace. It was high time she joined this particular discussion.

'Demetrius is a very busy man...' she began, but her voice was drowned out by Demetrius exclaiming that of course he would teach them. It might have to be later in the summer but...

'Can't we start now?' Rachel asked. 'I'd rather go snorkelling than play some silly games.'

'You've invited all your friends,' Demetrius said quietly. 'They're all waiting for the party to start.'

Chloe stepped forward, smiling. 'Would you like to organise a game, Rachel? There'll be plenty of time to swim another day.'

'OK, I'll start playing sardines,' Rachel said, rising to the occasion as she usually did. Raising her voice, she called, 'Come on everybody, over here! Close your eyes and count up to a hundred while I go and hide. No cheating! Then you can come and find me. When you find me you pile in beside me like sardines in a tin. First person to find me gets a prize, last person gets chucked in the water.'

'Last person gets a consolation prize, not a ducking in the water,' Samantha said quickly. 'Rachel was only joking.'

Rachel grinned at her sister. 'Was I?'

She scampered off as her little guests stood very still and closed their eyes.

Chloe glanced round at the children gathered on the terrace. The girls' frilly party frocks would soon be crumpled and dirty when they started searching for Rachel. Chloe's bet was that Rachel would disappear into their large garden at the back of the house. But they would all be quite safe there, under the watchful eye of Manolis who'd promised to guard their little guests.

Chloe smiled as she watched her daughter disappearing into the house. Rachel could be a little terror one minute and an angel the next. She loved her to bits! Feisty, full of fun, noisy! And Samantha was equally lovable in a completely different way. Her calm, quiet manner concealed a naturally happy character who exuded a caring warmth towards everyone she met.

Chloe looked up at Demetrius. He put out his hand and took hold of hers. For a few moments she remained very still, allowing herself to imagine what life would be like now if she'd not gone back to England. If Demetrius had wanted her to stay, she would have stayed. The twins would have been born here on this island instead of miles away from their real father.

Demetrius squeezed her hand. 'Are you all right, Chloe?' he whispered.

Gently she detached her hand and brought herself back to the present delicate situation. Her mother was at the centre of a group of parents, charming them with anecdotes of when the twins had been small. The parents were also anxious to chip in with stories of their own children, but a couple of the mothers in the group seemed more interested in watching Chloe and Demetrius.

They must be intrigued by the fact that the new doctor on the island had been invited to the party. She could imagine what they might be thinking. Perhaps Chloe had known him before? Perhaps he was a family friend?

'I ought to get the drinks flowing for the parents, Demetrius,' Chloe said quickly. 'So, if you'll excuse me...'

'Let me help you,' Demetrius said. 'Rachel and Samantha are doing a great job of organising their little friends. When you're eight you often prefer to be left to get on with it without your parents interfering.'

'Demetrius, please, don't talk about yourself as a parent,' Chloe said. 'Not yet. Soon, when—'

'I'm not going to,' he said, under his breath. 'I'm simply a colleague from the hospital who's helping you entertain your guests.'

He followed her into the sitting room, to the drinks table that Manolis and Maria had set out earlier. There were two bottles of champagne that hadn't been there earlier when Chloe had checked the table. The champagne had been set in an ice cooler that she hadn't seen before either. So that was why Demetrius had made two journeys back to his car after he'd arrived.

'My contribution to the festivities,' Demetrius said quietly, as he reached for one of the bottles and deftly removed the cork.

'Thank you,' Chloe said, as she took the glass he was holding out towards her. He poured a glass for himself and held it momentarily against hers.

'To our beautiful daughters,' he whispered, in a gentle husky tone.

Chloe could feel tears pricking behind her eyes. She could never have dreamed of such a wonderful moment, because she'd always accepted that Demetrius would never be the acknowledged father of her daughters. But now everything had changed.

But had Demetrius changed? If he'd gone to the trouble of coming to see her father all those years ago, why had he then proceeded to break her heart so soon afterwards? Looking up at him now, he looked so sincere. She could honestly believe him now if he said he loved her that it might mean for ever.

She took a sip of her champagne. 'I was afraid of what might happen if you came to the party. But now I'm glad you did.'

'So am I.' He put down his drink and reached forward to take her in his arms. For a moment they stayed so close that Chloe could feel Demetrius's heart beating against her breast.

'Can you get away later?' Demetrius whispered in her ear. 'Just the two of us. We have so much to celebrate by ourselves.'

Chloe groaned. 'Demetrius, don't tempt me…'

'Why not?' He gave her a rakish grin. 'Our daughters are enjoying their special day. Why shouldn't we?'

'Darling, I…' Chloe stopped as she realised she'd fallen back into her old ways so easily. She'd always called Demetrius 'darling' before but that had been different. To-day was today when there was too much at stake.

'Demetrius, you still haven't explained exactly what happened when you saw my father. I need to know. I need…'

He touched her face with a tender caress. 'Later, Chloe. Don't worry, I'll explain everything.'

As the last of the parents and children drove off down the road that skirted the bay, Chloe sank down into a chair in the sitting room. This was the one room in the house that her mother had made typically English in décor. Pam had arranged to have most of the furniture shipped out from England.

There were a couple of squashy sofas covered in a dark red, dramatic fabric. The comfy armchairs by contrast were in a cream-coloured cotton which matched the curtains, tied back beside the windows. They could be anywhere in the English countryside except when you looked out through the French windows onto the stone terrace. The view over the sea and beyond to the hills was typically Greek.

Chloe eased off her sandals and curled her feet under her. 'I'm really glad birthdays only come once a year, Mum.'

'Clever of you to have both your children on the same day,' Pam said, smiling across the room at her daughter. 'I'm so glad Anthony was able to get back in time to watch them blowing out the candles on their cakes.'

Chloe smiled. 'Yes, that was fun, wasn't it? I think everybody enjoyed the whole afternoon, don't you, Mum?'

'It was wonderful! I must say, I enjoy my grandchildren's parties more than I enjoyed my children's!' Pam paused. 'Anthony tells me he wants to discuss something medical with Demetrius so that's why he's asked him to stay on for a while. They're out on the terrace now, but when I went to speak to him just now they seemed to be discussing fishing.'

'I expect they'll get around to the medical talk sooner or later. Although I think Dad just likes an excuse to have another man about the place occasionally,' Chloe said lightly.

'Well, they do seem to be getting on rather well.'

'That's nice.'

She could feel her pulse rate increasing as, through the open French windows, she could see her father and Demetrius walking towards the sitting room.

'Come and sit beside me, Anthony,' Pam said, patting the cushions on the sofa.

'We're going to my study,' her husband said. 'Serious medical talk now. We also need Chloe to join us, if she will. The input of an experienced nursing sister is crucial to our discussion.'

'I was a nursing sister, remember,' Pam said, pretending to be put out that she was to be excluded from the discussion. 'Maybe I could help you as well.'

Anthony smiled. 'Too many cooks spoil the broth. Chloe will be adequate for the moment. If we need your expert opinion, I'll come and get you.'

He leaned forward and kissed his wife's cheek.

'Well, don't keep Demetrius and Chloe too long in your study, Anthony. They were in the hospital all morning and chasing around after the children this afternoon. It's time they had a break.'

'I'll remember that, Pam,' Anthony said, as he led the way out of the sitting room towards the stairs that led to his study.

As her father closed the door behind them Chloe felt as nervous as she had done on her first interview for a place in nursing school. She sank down in the armchair near the door, the furthest away from her father's desk.

She rarely came in this room but whenever she did she enjoyed the quiet ambience of the place. Her father had arranged for hand-crafted leather chairs to be brought over from Rhodes. A craftsman had constructed an intricately carved oak desk and fitted floor-to-ceiling bookshelves for Anthony's vast collection of books, some of which sat in piles, waiting for a space on the crowded shelves.

She tried to draw comfort from the peaceful atmosphere. She breathed in the scent of the leather which had always fascinated her on previous happier occasions. But, try as she would, she found herself fighting against the nervous apprehension which threatened to overwhelm her.

'Dad, it's all been a bit of a shock to me, finding out that—' she began nervously.

'Come a bit closer, Chloe,' Anthony broke in, waving a hand towards the chair beside his desk. 'That's better. We need to be in a group for a group discussion, don't we?'

Demetrius had already seated himself in front of the desk and was sitting bolt upright on a hard-backed chair. He cleared his throat nervously.

'With the greatest respect, sir, I think Chloe is feeling as nervous as I am, so could you come to the point of the discussion as quickly as possible?'

Chloe held her breath. Nobody hurried Anthony Metcalfe! He was used to handling junior doctors who didn't know their place.

Anthony began speaking in a subdued voice. 'I was very impressed by the fact that you came to see me before, Demetrius, all those years ago. It must have taken great courage to ask for my daughter's hand in marriage when you knew we were all hoping she would marry Patrick.'

'I thought there was a good chance that Chloe was going to stay here on the island with me.'

'But she didn't, and now things are much more complicated,' Anthony said. 'When are you going to tell Rachel and Samantha? And what about Chloe's mother? Which is why I asked you to come here today, Demetrius. My wife was very fond of Patrick. His mother was one of her oldest friends. Patrick was Pam's godson. It would break her heart if she thought that—'

'No it won't break Mum's heart,' Chloe said, with a confidence that belied the butterflies in her stomach. 'Initially she'll be upset, but she'll accept the new situation as time goes by.'

She took a deep breath to steady herself. 'Mum is a very strong character. But I agree with you that we shouldn't upset Mum just yet. She's got a lot on her plate, organising

Sara's wedding. I don't want to spoil her enjoyment as mother of the bride and I don't want Sara to have to worry about Mum at this crucial time either. As soon as the wedding is over, when Sara and Michaelis have gone off on honeymoon, I'll tell Mum myself and—'

'Now, just wait a minute!' Demetrius's voice was steely. 'I know I promised Chloe I would keep our secret till after the wedding but, seeing my daughters this afternoon, knowing how we've already bonded, don't you think my feelings need to be considered?'

Chloe looked across at Demetrius and her heart went out to him as she saw the distress in his moist, dark eyes. Behind his strong, confident manner there was a deep sadness. She glanced at her father but he was sitting with an anguished expression on his face, twisting his fountain pen nervously in his hand.

'Demetrius, we know it's hard for you,' he began, but Demetrius got to his feet.

'Hard! It's impossible!'

He moved purposefully towards the door, turning in the doorway to look at Anthony. 'I'm sorry we weren't able to come to an agreement.'

'Demetrius!' Chloe was on her feet, running across the study with her arms outstretched. 'Please, don't go. Come back and we'll talk some more. There must be a solution…'

'Goodbye, Chloe.'

As the door closed behind him, Chloe covered her face with her hands. Her father got up from the desk to put an arm round the heaving shoulders.

'Don't cry, Chloe. You've coped so well on your own before.'

Anthony put his hand into his pocket and took out a large white handkerchief.

'But that was different.' Chloe said, wiping her eyes with her father's hanky. 'That was when I was alone. Now I've got Demetrius to consider as well. I can't bear to hurt him any more than I already have.'

For a moment Anthony hesitated. 'Are you still in love with Demetrius?'

'Yes… I always was… I always will be.'

'In that case, I'll do everything I can to help you. All I've ever wanted since you were born is that you should be happy. But…'

Anthony broke off, looking down at his daughter with troubled eyes. 'Let's take it one step at a time. I always suspected that Demetrius might be the father of our darling granddaughters, but I never said anything to your mother. We both know how much she loved Patrick. Once Sara's wedding is over, you can tell her everything…and I'll help you through what could be a very difficult time.'

Chloe wiped her eyes and smiled up at her father. 'Thanks, Dad. You know…' She hesitated. 'I wish I'd confided in you before. When I came out here with you and Mum when I was twenty, I thought I had to keep everything to myself. I knew I had to sort out my feelings for Patrick before the end of the summer, but I just couldn't bring myself to ask anybody for advice. I knew Mum was simply taking it for granted that we would get engaged soon and—'

'Chloe, it's OK,' Anthony said gently. 'Come and sit over here where we'll be more comfortable.'

Chloe sank down in a comfy leather armchair near her father.

Anthony cleared his throat but it was still croaky when he spoke. 'Ever since you were a little girl, I've noticed that you kept things to yourself. Sara is more open. Francesca is just like you. I never know what she's thinking. But I know that when you've thought your problem through you'll usually tell me what's worrying you. In the case of you and Demetrius, it's taken eight years for you to confide in me. But now that you have, I want you to know that I'm here for you.'

Chloe swallowed hard. 'Thanks, Dad. There were times when I wanted to confide in you, but I'd promised Patrick I wouldn't.'

'I understand. From now on, you must feel free to tell me as little or as much as you want but, please, not a word to Mum until after Sara's wedding. It won't be easy to explain to the twins either. But they were only three months old when Patrick died so he didn't figure largely in their lives. You used to show them photos of Patrick and talk about him but...' Anthony hesitated. 'From what I've seen of Demetrius, I think the twins will be overjoyed to know he's their father.'

Chloe smiled. 'So do I. They seem, in some intuitive way, to have bonded with Demetrius already.'

Anthony nodded. 'I noticed that, too.' He leaned across and kissed her cheek. 'We mustn't rush things. Let's take one step at a time, eh?'

CHAPTER FIVE

As CHLOE lifted baby Vasilio from his cot beside Nicoletta's bed she couldn't help remembering how she'd helped Demetrius to deliver him three weeks ago, on the twins' birthday. Because Vasilio shared a birthday with the twins and because she and Demetrius had been together at the birth, this dear little baby held a special place in her heart.

It seemed like a lifetime since she'd been close to Demetrius. They'd worked together at the hospital. They'd delivered more babies together and discussed patients together in a perfectly professional, civilised way. But the steely calm behind Demetrius's voice when he spoke to her was enough to make her want to weep.

There had been no personal communication between them at all, and Chloe was beginning to feel that she couldn't take much more. When the twins had asked her that morning when Demetrius was going to come over and start teaching them to snorkel with the equipment he'd brought them on their birthday, she'd had to tell them once more that Demetrius was a very busy doctor who'd just started a new job at the hospital. She'd told them that she hoped he would be able to see more of them later in the summer when he had more time.

And as Chloe had kissed Rachel and Samantha goodbye, she'd found herself actually counting the weeks to Sara's wedding. Suddenly August couldn't come round soon enough!

She handed over baby Vasilio to Nicoletta, who was

sitting in an armchair beside her bed. The young mum smiled as she placed her infant son against her breast.

'My breasts are quite free of that infection now, Sister. It doesn't hurt a bit when I feed Vasilio. You know, I'm almost glad I got that mastitis, or whatever it's called, in the right breast. It was painful at first but it meant I could stay in here a bit longer. I honestly didn't want to go home to my mother-in-law. Costas has been off on the boats again for the last two weeks and it would have been awful on my own with her.'

Chloe nodded knowingly. 'I know, families, eh? Problems, always problems!'

Nicoletta pulled a wry face. 'My mother-in-law has known me since I was a little girl. She still thinks I'm a child who can't manage her own life.'

'Is there a chance you and Costas could get a place of your own?'

'Costas is hoping to rent a little house in the upper town when the present owners move away,' Nicoletta said, moving her baby from one breast to the other. 'When he gets back from his present working trip in two days' time, he's promised to put down the deposit that's needed before we can move in.'

'Well, that's good news.' Chloe hesitated. She'd become very fond of this particular patient in the three weeks she'd been in hospital and she didn't want to upset her. 'Actually, I've been going to suggest that now the inflammation in your breast has cleared up, you should be able to leave hospital. If Costas arrives back in two days' time I'll be able to discharge you, Nicoletta.'

'You've been so good, looking after me, Chloe. Yes, I'll be OK to leave in a couple of days.'

Chloe made a mental note to write that in her report. It was good to see Nicoletta looking so fit. Now that the mastitis had cleared up and she was happy about her home arrangements, which had been part of the reason why they'd kept her so long, her patient would continue to get stronger. She moved off down the ward towards the delivery room. There was a patient whose delivery might need speeding up. The foetus seemed reluctant to get moving. The obstetric team needed to decide whether intervention was going to be necessary.

Arriving at the delivery suite, she went into the small room at the side of the first delivery room. The patient she'd been going to see was lying on the bed on one side of the room. Demetrius was standing beside her, setting up an IV.

'I've decided to hurry things along, Chloe, so I'm fixing up this oxytocin IV.' he said, without looking up from his task. 'The foetus is beginning to show signs of distress.'

'Yes, I was thinking that might be necessary,' Chloe said. 'Would you like me to stay and—?'

'No need,' Demetrius told her in the super-efficient professional voice he'd been using for the past three weeks. 'Your excellent midwives have been most helpful. I'm sure you need to get back to your duties on the ward.'

Chloe turned and hurried away.

'Sister, can I ask you about my baby?' one of the patients called. 'Do you think she's getting enough milk?'

Chloe went over to the bed, almost relieved to be needed again. For the rest of the morning, her attention was wholly taken up with looking after her patients and keeping the ward running smoothly.

At the end of the morning she decided not to go down to the dining room for lunch. She could send out for a piece of spanakopita, delicious spinach pie, from the bakery down at the harbour and stay at her desk to catch up with some of her paperwork. That way, she could get away on time this evening to go back to Rachel and Samantha. They would have one of their lovely evenings together, maybe starting with a swim down by the jetty.

She picked up her phone and got through to Reception. 'Oh, hello, Michelle, this is Chloe. Have you a messenger or a porter free down there? I need somebody to nip out to the bakery and...' She listened. 'Oh, I see, you've got a temporary receptionist who's free...'

The helpful Australian receptionist told Chloe that when the new receptionist got back from her latest errand she would send her out to the bakery.

'Diana only started this morning and she's learning the ropes,' Michelle said. 'But if you're prepared to wait...'

Chloe proceeded to give her order for the spanakopita over the phone before sitting down at her desk and beginning to sort through the mound of case notes and letters. What she needed was a secretary! Maybe she could persuade Michaelis to lend her the services of Panayota for a couple of hours a week. Unlikely! Michaelis didn't enjoy paperwork either and he kept his secretary fully occupied.

She looked up as she heard a tap on the door, relieved to be interrupted in her boring task. She'd been working nearly half an hour so hopefully it was her lunch. They'd said the girl was learning but she'd had time to gather the spinach and bake some spanakopita, never mind fetching it from the bakery!

'Come in!'

Demetrius was already walking into her office. 'I came to give you some details about our latest delivery for your report,' he began in a cool voice, putting his hands on the edge of her desk.

Chloe looked up at him. 'Demetrius, how long are you going to keep up this cold war?'

'Cold war! That's rich, coming from you.' He moved

his hands from the desk and pulled himself to his full height. 'You and your family have made it quite clear that I'm not wanted. You have—'

'That's not true, Demetrius. We've asked you to be patient about—'

'This isn't something I can be patient about, Chloe,' Demetrius said heatedly. 'How much more of my daughters' lives are you going to steal from me? How long do you think—?'

'Sister, have you got my baby in here?'

The door burst open and a distressed Nicoletta hurried up to the desk.

'Why would I bring Vasilio in here, Nicoletta? I thought he was with you in the ward.'

'I put him in the nursery about half an hour ago so that I could go out into the garden for some fresh air. The nurse in charge said she'd keep an eye on him. But when I got back the cot I'd put him in was empty. The nurse said she'd been called away for a couple of minutes and when she got back... Oh, Sister, what are we going to do?'

Chloe's years of experience clicked in. First rule of nursing—don't panic, well, at least not in front of the patient. Her heart was pounding. She'd become very fond of little Vasilio—too fond, probably. It was difficult to remain detached and professional in a situation like this. She could imagine only too well how she would feel if this was her own baby who was missing.

'Vasilio must be in the building somewhere,' she said in a confident, unwavering tone.

'Let's go to the nursery and see the nurse who was supposed to be looking after the baby,' Demetrius said quickly. 'Come on, we mustn't waste a second.'

The young junior nurse was adamant that she'd only left the nursery for a couple of minutes.

'I needed to make a phone call,' the girl said anxiously. 'This new receptionist had just brought up some stationery. She was actually having a look around the nursery at the time. Said she loved babies and was thinking of changing her job and working with them. So I just asked her to keep an eye on the babies till I got back. They were all healthy babies in the nursery. No problems at all so I thought it would be OK. When I got back and saw the empty cot where Vasilio had been, I simply thought his mum had taken him.'

'You should never assume anything, Nurse,' Chloe said, hardening her heart so that she could teach this junior nurse a valuable lesson. 'You should always check and double-check everything.'

'This receptionist you spoke about,' Demetrius began carefully. 'You say she's new to the job.'

'Never seen her before today, Doctor. Tall, thin, dark-haired, talked good English but looks Greek.'

Chloe felt a shiver run down her spine. The temporary receptionist, newly appointed today. Looking round the nursery. Taking her time.

'I'm going back to my office, Demetrius,' she said, quickly. 'I want to check if my lunch has arrived.'

Demetrius hurried along the corridor beside her. 'Chloe, this is no time to worry about lunch. Don't you think—?'

'I'll explain in a moment. Come into the office with me. I've got one of my most sympathetic nurses taking care of Nicoletta in the side ward. The important thing is to check up on this so-called receptionist.'

She sank down at the desk and picked up the phone. This time Demetrius was not only leaning on the desk, he had one hand on her shoulder as if to steady her. It was comforting to feel the touch of his fingers again.

'Hello, Michelle? This is Chloe. I'm still waiting for my

spanakopita. Has Diana…? She hasn't got back yet from her previous errand? Put me through to Security. Meanwhile, don't let anyone in or out of the hospital. One of our babies is missing. Have all the doors closed now…yes, now, as in immediately!'

Chloe's second phone rang.

'Security here! How can I…?'

Chloe quickly explained that a baby had gone missing. She suspected that the new temporary receptionist might have taken him. Would they, please, search the building? Also, they should get somebody to notify the police.

'May I speak to Security?' Demetrius asked, reaching forward to take the phone from Chloe.

'You can get a full description of the suspect from Michelle in Reception. Her first name is Diana,' Demetrius told the security guard. 'Ask the police to circulate this as soon as possible.'

He put down the phone.

'It's all so worrying,' Chloe said. Leaning back in her chair, she realised that Demetrius was still standing close behind her. She turned and looked up into his dark, sympathetic eyes. Oh, how she'd missed that expression on his face during the last three weeks when he'd looked at her as if she were a complete stranger!

'It's out of our hands now,' Demetrius said. 'Security will do a thorough search of the building, but my guess is that this Diana will probably have got out of the hospital by now. She could be anywhere.'

'She'll find it hard to leave the island,' Chloe said.

Demetrius moved around to sit beside her at the desk. Unbidden, he reached out his hand and took hold of hers in a comforting gesture.

'On the other hand, if she has access to a small fishing

boat, she could leave the island from any number of tiny inlets in the coast, Demetrius,' Chloe said softly.

'I know,' Demetrius said. 'I was hoping you wouldn't think about that. The police will know they've got a tremendous task on their hands.'

'But isn't there something we can do?'

Demetrius shook his head. 'Leave it to the police. We can stop worrying in front of the patients and keep on working as normal.'

The long afternoon wore on. Chloe was beside herself with anxiety yet she managed to maintain an air of professionalism and calm on the ward. She took care of the new baby which Demetrius had delivered soon after setting up the oxytocin IV. In spite of having suffered some distress when the mother's contractions had been sluggish, the baby was fine and healthy now.

'She's a strong baby,' Chloe told the mother as the baby began suckling.

'Got a healthy appetite as well,' the mother said proudly. 'Sister, what's all this I've been hearing about a baby snatch?'

The news had spread like wildfire and the patients were talking of nothing else. Chloe did her best to reassure the patient that all steps were being taken to find the baby and to make sure it didn't happen again. She had to repeat her message so many times she realised she would have to make a general announcement soon. All the mothers were understandably refusing to let their babies out of their sight.

Going down the corridor that ran the full length of the floor she was in charge of, she called in at each ward, asked for everyone's attention and then slowly and carefully explained what had happened. After that she answered all the questions that the patients and staff put to her. As she went back to her office she felt that the atmosphere in her section of the hospital was now much calmer.

But, going into her office and settling herself at her desk, she was feeling anything but calm. It was difficult to concentrate on writing the report she would have to give to Kate. Chloe got up and fixed herself a cup of coffee before applying herself to her task once more.

Minutes later, she was surprised to see Kate walk into the office.

'You're not due till five, Kate.'

'I know, but I wanted to get here and see if there's any news of the missing baby. Everybody on the island is talking about it.'

Chloe shook her head. 'No news, I'm afraid. I keep ringing Security and the police but they tell me they'll let me know as soon as anything happens. I've almost finished the report. Would you like a coffee?'

'I'll get it. You finish your writing, Chloe.' Kate picked up the cafetière from the hot plate in the corner of the room.

The door opened. 'Can you spare a cup for a poor exhausted doctor?'

Kate smiled at Demetrius. 'Of course we can. Any news of—?'

'If anybody else asks me if there's any news—!'

Demetrius sank down on a chair near the door. 'I'd love to phone Security again, but they sounded a bit annoyed last time.'

'That's because everybody's ringing at the same time,' Chloe said, setting down her cup. 'I feel so helpless here. I want to be out there, searching for this Diana woman. She hasn't been seen since my nurse saw her in the nursery so Diana has got to be the culprit. She's tall, with long dark hair, speaks good English but looks Greek, the nurse said.'

'Well, that should narrow the field,' Demetrius said wryly as he turned to look at Kate. 'You'll be in charge when Sister goes off duty, won't you, Kate? Would you mind if Chloe comes with me now so that we can do our own search? It's so frustrating to be waiting. I'm technically off duty now. There's a good obstetric team already on duty for the evening work so...'

'I don't mind at all if you both go off and search,' Katerina said. 'I'm here now so I'd like to be useful.'

Chloe smiled. 'Thanks, Kate.' She glanced at Demetrius. 'Excellent idea! I'll just give Kate my written report and answer her questions before we go.'

Chloe and Demetrius mingled with the tourists and the Ceres residents along the harbourside. Now that they were actually away from hospital, their plan of finding the missing baby Vasilio and his abductor didn't seem to be such a brilliant idea.

'Like looking for a needle in a haystack,' Chloe said as she walked along the quayside, staring at each of the yachts and boats tied up there.

'A needle in a haystack?' Demetrius repeated in a puzzled tone. 'Why would you want to find a needle in—?'

'It's an old English saying. What it means is—'

'Look at that boat there!' Demetrius broke in excitedly. 'See the small pram? No baby in it but—'

'There's a lady bringing the baby out of the cabin now,' Chloe said, holding her breath as a figure emerged.

'A blonde woman,' Demetrius said dejectedly, as the small, smartly dressed woman appeared.

'And the baby's blond as well,' Chloe whispered.

'And it looks at least six months old,' Demetrius said.

The woman looked directly at the staring couple of strangers beside her boat on the quayside. She smiled and held out the baby so they could get a better look.

'It's OK, the police have already been here,' the woman said in a friendly tone. 'They've been on every boat in the harbour. We've all heard about the missing baby. Are you friends of the mother?'

'Yes, we are,' Demetrius said, quickly, not wanting to divulge too much information. 'Thanks for being so helpful.'

They moved on. Walking beside Demetrius now, Chloe could imagine they were taking a leisurely stroll. Demetrius, in jeans and open-necked shirt, looked relaxed and carefree, his expression belying the concern he was feeling. Chloe, too, had changed, into a cool cotton pale blue gingham dress buttoned down the front. She could have passed for a tourist on holiday.

But the pain and anxiety of losing baby Vasilio was weighing her down. It was comforting to have Demetrius beside her. It was the first time he'd been civil towards her since the discussion with her father had ended in Demetrius walking out.

She'd been into the side ward to see how Nicoletta was bearing up before she left hospital. Demetrius had come with her and offered his support. Nicoletta was a tough young woman but the burden of not knowing who had carried off her precious baby was taking its toll. Chloe thought of Nicoletta now, remembering how she'd left her red-eyed and silently staring out of the window, watching the harbourside as if she hoped to suddenly catch a glimpse of little Vasilio. She would still be sitting up there in hospital now, poor girl.

Somebody had to find her baby before it was too late!

'Hello, Chloe!'

Chloe turned at the sound of a vaguely familiar voice. 'Vanessa! When did you get back?'

The tall, striking, auburn-haired woman smiled. 'A couple of days ago. Don't get to Ceres very much now. Haven't seen you for years.'

Chloe smiled at her old friend. 'Demetrius, you remember Vanessa, don't you?'

Demetrius nodded. 'Hello, Vanessa. We can't stop. We're on hospital business.'

'I suppose you're looking for that baby who's gone missing. Everybody's talking about it. Nice to see you both again. We must get together some time. I'm over here for a few weeks, trying to sell my dad's house. We hardly use it now so—'

'I'm really sorry, but we've got to go, Vanessa,' Chloe said, feeling Demetrius's hand under her arm pulling her away.

As they edged their way through the crowd gathered along the quayside, Chloe reflected that she hadn't seen Vanessa for eight years. Vanessa had been the only person who'd known about her affair with Demetrius and she'd been particularly helpful. She must try to see her again when she could find the time. But for the present all she could think about was Vasilio. As a mother herself she couldn't begin to imagine the anguish Nicoletta must be going through.

As she heard the sound of the horn blowing from the four o'clock ferry nearby her anxiety about little Vasilio increased. He couldn't possibly have been smuggled onto the ferry, could he? The police would have checked and double-checked the passengers.

The crew of the huge boat was preparing to set sail. People were hanging over the side of the boat from the upper deck, waving goodbye to their friends.

Everyone was a friend on Ceres, and perfect strangers would wave to the departing passengers.

'I suppose you've thoroughly checked all the passengers, Officer?' Demetrius said in Greek to a young policeman who was watching the preparations for the departure of the ferry.

'A very thorough search was conducted.' He narrowed his eyes as he took in Demetrius's casual clothes. 'Are you involved with this baby that's gone missing?'

'I'm the doctor who brought him into the world,' Demetrius said quietly. 'And this is the sister who assisted me.'

'That's why he's so special to us,' Chloe said, her voice cracking with emotion.

She watched a family of latecomers hurrying to the boat. Looked like mother, father, two young sons and a baby in a pram. Only a couple of minutes to go. They were cutting it fine.

The young policeman stepped forward to speak to the man, who was pushing the pram. Chloe moved nearer. The father was tall and dark, but the mother was small and blonde. The hood of the pram was up. Was that to shield the baby from the sun or...?

The crowd was surging forward. Chloe couldn't get close enough. The policeman, obviously satisfied, was telling the family they could board. The ferry horn sounded its final loud blast, which echoed across the harbour.

'Just a minute!' Demetrius grabbed Chloe's hand as he pushed his way through the crowd.

Chloe heard someone shouting to Demetrius that they couldn't board the ship as she followed him, still clinging to his hand. An angry sailor was trying to prevent Demetrius from boarding. She stood her ground with him. Demetrius must have seen something the others hadn't.

'That family over there. I need to speak to them,' Demetrius said in a loud, authoritative voice.

Chloe found she was trembling. The father of the family turned away, raising his hands to his face. In a split second Chloe realised what had alerted Demetrius to the fact that this was no ordinary family. The hands of the person supposed to be the father were thin and well manicured, apart from the chipped nail varnish that looked as if someone had hastily tried to remove it.

And these hands were extremely feminine!

Demetrius pushed the sailor aside. Chloe clung tightly to his hand as they reached the suspicious-looking person. She could now detect small strands of freshly cut hair sticking to the collar of the man's jacket. Everything pointed to the fact that the impostor had recently had a short masculine-type haircut.

'You're Diana, aren't you?' Demetrius said quietly, before raising his voice. 'Over here, Officer!'

Four policemen hurried onto the ferry as the now terrified Diana started screaming hysterically. Chloe bent over the pram and looked at the baby. There was no mistaking the adorable little Vasilio. She picked him up and held him close. He blinked but didn't waken up. There was dried milk at the side of his mouth. Someone had obviously fed him recently.

The two boys of this strange family group started crying. 'What's happening, Mum?' the older of the two asked to the small blonde woman. 'You didn't say this was going to happen. You said you were going to buy us some—'

'Keep your mouth shut, you little…' The woman glanced around her as one of the policemen took hold of her arm.

'You'd all better come off the boat now,' one of the

policemen said in a firm, no-nonsense voice. 'We can't hold the passengers up any longer. This way, please.'

Diana was now screaming abuse at the police but nobody was showing any concern for her as the distraught woman and her accomplices were led off the ferry. The policeman who'd first spoken to Demetrius and Chloe, having radioed the hospital for confirmation that they really were a doctor and sister on the lookout for the baby, told them that a full-scale investigation into the hospital and the medical staff who had allowed this to happen would be started immediately.

He asked them to take the baby back to the hospital and assured them that the police would deal with the people concerned in the abduction and find out exactly what they'd intended to do with the stolen baby.

An ambulance was now arriving on the quayside. The hospital must have sent it. Chloe held baby Vasilio tightly in her arms. He snuggled against her, his little mouth snuffling against her cotton top.

'You'll soon be back with your mummy, Vasilio,' she whispered.

In the back of the ambulance, Demetrius put his arm round her. Vasilio was asleep, lying in a cot fixed to the side of the ambulance, totally oblivious to what was going on around him. Chloe shivered. She wasn't sure if it was the exhaustion or the feel of Demetrius's arm around her, but she felt positively light-headed.

Back at the hospital, there was an emotional reunion of mother and baby. Nicoletta was hysterical with relief. As Chloe brought the baby to her, Nicoletta began to scream and sob uncontrollably.

'Vasilio, oh, my baby, my baby!'

Nicoletta was holding out her arms towards her son, but

Chloe, afraid that Nicoletta was still too distraught, partially held onto the baby as his mother's arms clasped him.

'Vasilio, Vasilio!' Nicoletta was now cradling her baby against her, but her voice sounded calmer.

Chloe removed her own hands but still stood close to Nicoletta, who took one hand away from her baby to wipe the tears from her eyes.

'Thank you, oh, thank you, Chloe, and you, too, Demetrius.' Nicoletta was breathing deeply to calm herself. 'Do we know why that woman took Vasilio away?'

'Not yet, Nicoletta,' Demetrius said. 'The police have started a full-scale investigation into how this was allowed to happen. Now, we want you to take things easy for the next few days. You've had a terrible shock and you need to gather your strength. Chloe has instructed one of the nurses to stay with you all the time to help care for you and baby Vasilio.'

Chloe went back to her office when she was satisfied that everything possible was being done for Nicoletta and baby Vasilio. Sitting at her desk, writing a brief report of Vasilio's abduction, Chloe found her thoughts constantly turning to Rachel and Samantha. How would she have felt if one of her own babies had been abducted? She felt a pang of anguish run through her. Unable to concentrate any more, she picked up the phone. She wanted to make sure that her own children were safe and sound. She wanted to hear the sound of their little voices, to tell them she would soon be home and...

'Oh, hi, Mum, it's Chloe. Can I speak to Rachel and Samantha?'

'Sorry, Chloe, they're not here.'

Chloe felt her heart turn over. Not there!

'Where are they? Are they OK?'

'Of course they're OK. They've been invited to a sleep-over party at one of their friends' houses. They forgot to mention it until they were getting into the car to go to school. I had to dash back into the house and pack up their pyjamas and toothbrushes. I hope you don't mind me saying they could go at such short notice.'

'No, they would have been disappointed if we hadn't let them go.'

She glanced across the office as Demetrius walked in. He was mouthing something that looked very much like, 'When are you going to be free?'

'Are you all right, Chloe? You sound a bit worried.'

'Oh, it's been a difficult day, Mum, that's all. We had an emergency here and—'

'Yes, I heard about it on the radio just now. Apparently the police have got the baby back, haven't they?'

'They have, thank goodness!'

'Were you involved in the rescue?'

'I suppose you could say that. It was something of a team effort at the end.'

It would take too long to explain. She looked across at Demetrius. He was looking just like his old self, wonderfully relaxed.

'Mum, can you tell me where Rachel and Samantha are staying tonight? I need to see them.'

'I've got the phone number. You could phone them if you like.'

'I...I'd rather see them face to face.'

Chloe listened as her mother explained where the twins were staying. 'Yes, I can find it. The large house with the green shutters on the first street after the bakery. Thanks, Mum. See you later.'

As she put down the phone she looked at Demetrius, who was leaning across her desk.

'I wanted to speak to Rachel and Samantha,' she said quietly. 'But they're spending the night with some friends, so...'

Demetrius stood up and came round the desk, pulling her to her feet so that he could hold her against him.

'You just want to reassure yourself that your own babies are fine, don't you?' he asked.

Her voice choked as she replied, 'I need to see them.'

'Of course you do. So do I.'

Demetrius put his hands on each side of her face and drew her lips towards him. Gently, he kissed her, waiting to feel some response. When he did, he dared to draw her closer, feeling the soft contours of her body moulding against his.

'I've missed you so much, Chloe,' he whispered as he held her close.

He could feel her trembling. He hoped she was feeling as moved as he was by this much-desired reunion. If Chloe only knew how he'd longed to hold her like this over the last three weeks! Even though he'd stormed away from her house after the meeting with her father, his feelings for Chloe had not changed.

In the long hours of his sleepless nights he'd thought about the tragic way she'd rejected him eight years ago. It had been so unexpected. But now, meeting up with her after all these years, realising that she'd borne him two beautiful daughters, couldn't he dare to hope that she might now feel differently?

The man she'd left him for was no longer alive. Chloe was the mother of his children. She should have been his wife by now. He felt he ought to have been more forceful with her father, but he had great respect for Anthony Metcalfe and he didn't want to make things difficult for Chloe at home.

If only he could be sure that Chloe had changed, that she loved him as she'd appeared to love him during that wonderful summer. But he couldn't be sure she wouldn't break his heart again. And that was why he'd put on this façade of indifference during the last three weeks.

Oh, it had been so difficult, working with Chloe! Obstetrics involved more than mere mechanics. Your whole self was involved when you were delivering babies. And looking across the delivery table at Chloe whenever she held a small, perfectly formed, infinitely exquisite newborn infant in her arms had been too poignant for words. He remembered positively scowling at her one day and making a critical remark just so that he wouldn't find himself reaching out towards her and begging her to return to him.

But today, involved in the heart-rending search for the missing baby, he'd realised that they had to get together as a family, and as soon as possible. The rest of the world didn't matter. The sooner he and Chloe were a family unit, the better.

'Chloe, let me take you to see the twins.'

Chloe hesitated, but the feel of Demetrius's comforting arms around her convinced her. 'Yes…I'd like that.'

He loosened his embrace. 'And when you've reassured yourself that you've got two wonderful healthy little girls who love you to bits, let me take you home where we can relax. Just the two of us. I'll make some supper. We've both had a hard day and—'

'Home? Where do you mean?'

He smiled. 'You surely haven't forgotten my house, the place you said had come to feel like home?'

Chloe looked perplexed. 'You mean your house in Chorio? But I thought you would have sold it when you went to Australia.'

'A distant cousin was getting married so I let him have the house at a peppercorn rent. He moved over to Rhodes about six months ago. That was about the time my divorce was finalised. I started to feel homesick. There was nothing to keep me in Australia so I applied for a job at the hospital and came back to Ceres. I'm only just getting the place in shape. I think it needs a woman's touch.'

Chloe felt herself going weak as she listened to Demetrius's husky, passionate voice. This was how he used to talk to her, freely and frankly, laying himself completely open and holding nothing back.

'I'd like to see the house again,' she said quietly.

CHAPTER SIX

THE twins were delighted to see Demetrius and Chloe when they called in at the house where they were spending the night with their friend Natasha and several other little schoolfriends.

'Mum, what a surprise!' Rachel got down from the crowded, noisy supper table, closely followed by Samantha.

Chloe knelt down and hugged them both. Samantha smiled shyly at Demetrius and put out her little hand to pull him down from his great height. He gave her a kiss on the cheek. Rachel held up her cheek to be kissed.

'Why have you come, Demetrius?' Rachel said, grinning mischievously as she held onto the hand that Samantha wasn't holding.

Demetrius smiled. 'Well, that's a nice welcome, I must say!'

'Are you staying for the party?' Samantha asked. 'It's Natasha's birthday and her mum's made this enormous birthday cake and...'

As the twins talked to Demetrius, Chloe explained to Natasha's mother that she'd called in to make sure the twins had brought everything they needed for the night.

'Of course they have everything they need.' The young Greek mother smiled at Chloe. 'Their grandmother brought their pyjamas, toothbrushes, clean clothes for school to-morrow and a beautiful birthday present for my daughter. Your mother said the girls had forgotten to tell her about the party until this morning. I'm so glad they were able to come. Now, you and Dr Demetrius must stay and have a drink with us and—'

'You're very kind but I'm afraid we can't stay this evening. We've only just got off duty at the hospital and—'

'Of course! You must be very busy. Well, you are always welcome here. Another time perhaps.'

Outside the house, Chloe told Demetrius that she was glad they'd called in.

'What a lovely woman. So friendly, so understanding.'

'So Greek,' Demetrius said. 'So like most of the mothers on this island.'

Chloe smiled. 'Exactly! I feel so much happier now, so much more...'

'Reassured?'

Chloe nodded. 'After the awful events of today, I just wanted to thank my lucky stars that my children were safe.'

Demetrius put his arm lightly round her shoulders. 'I think you're a wonderful mum. Come on, let's go home.'

Chloe waited as Demetrius unlocked the ancient iron door that led into the small courtyard of his home. She remembered the intriguing old key that looked as if it had been used by countless owners of this house. For several hundred years, nobody had ever thought it necessary to change the locks between owners.

The people of Ceres were intrinsically very honest. Doors were often left unlocked. Nothing was ever stolen. The policemen sat around playing cards. Except today, when they'd had to spring into action.

'I hope the police will let us know soon what they find out about the woman who abducted Vasilio,' Chloe said, as she followed Demetrius through the quaint old enclosed courtyard into the beamed, low-ceilinged kitchen.

'So do I, but you must try to switch off from thinking about the hospital,' Demetrius said, turning to draw her against him. 'Tonight is just for us.'

Chloe sighed as she allowed herself to be folded into his embrace. Standing absolutely still in the deliciously sensual enclosure of Demetrius's arms, she could imagine that the clock had been turned back eight years. It looked as if the distant cousin that Demetrius had spoken about hadn't changed a thing, thank goodness!

Everything was just as she remembered it from that wonderful, carefree time when she'd been much younger and infinitely more trusting. The same shelves above the sink held the ageless saucepans, casseroles, glasses and plates that they'd used when they'd had long enough together to share the cooking of a clandestine lunch or supper during one of their secret trysts.

The wall cupboard with the glass front still held the fascinating array of antique wineglasses, tiny coffee-cups, fragile porcelain plates and bowls that had been so obviously rarely used over the last few years.

And on the wooden dresser near the sink was the home-made raffia basket that Chloe knew Demetrius had made at school to hold the embroidery that his mother had been working on the day she died.

She smiled dreamily as she moved away from Demetrius to touch the basket. Raising the lid, she saw that it was indeed exactly as she remembered it—skeins of brightly coloured silk, needles, small scissors, a tiny thimble.

There was a lump in her throat as she turned to look at Demetrius. 'I would have loved to have met your mother.'

'And she would have loved to have met you,' Demetrius said, his voice husky with emotion.

'I remember you said she was considered old when you were born.'

Demetrius nodded. 'Yes, my mother was in her late forties when she gave birth to me, her only child. My father was almost sixty. Both my parents were born in Athens. My father was a schoolmaster. He was a confirmed bachelor, he told me, until he met my mother. After they married they were hoping to have a family but it didn't happen. When my father decided to retire from teaching they moved to Ceres, bought this house and soon after that I came along.'

Chloe smiled. Demetrius had told her this story before but she'd wanted to hear it again. She enjoyed listening to the warmth in his voice when he spoke about his parents.

'Your mother and father must have been thrilled to have a baby when they'd waited so long.'

Demetrius's face broke into a boyish smile of happiness. Chloe could imagine the handsome young boy twisting his parents round his little finger.

'I bet you were spoiled rotten, Demetrius!'

'I was! All Greek boys are spoiled by their mothers but I was truly doted on. But you know, the funny thing is, I don't think it did me any harm. I think children need to know that they're loved and wanted, don't you, Chloe?'

She swallowed hard. 'The twins have always known they were loved by the whole of our family,' she said in a defensive tone. 'Patrick died when they were just three months old so they never had a father…a father figure in their lives…'

She broke off as she saw the closed expression on Demetrius's face. She didn't want to spoil the atmosphere so early in their evening together. She didn't want to have to make decisions that might create a contentious atmosphere.

Demetrius reached into the fridge and began opening a bottle of wine. His back towards her, he appeared to be totally involved with his task but Chloe suspected that, like her, he was biding his time before they discussed the really important issues. Like the twins, when they were going to be told that Demetrius was their father. Who was going to break the news? How would they react? How would the rest of the family react?

Chloe felt as if she was in limbo at the moment. This break in her normal life was giving her a chance to snatch a short time alone with Demetrius. So far, there had been nothing to spoil their time together this evening, but she knew that Demetrius wasn't happy with the current situation. Neither was she!

'Let's take our drinks onto the terrace,' Demetrius said, handing her a glass before opening the double doors that led out onto the wide stone terrace overlooking the hillside that led down to the sea.

Looking out over the ancient red-tiled rooftops of the picturesque houses in Chorio, Chloe could just make out the tiny stretch of water in Nimborio Bay where she lived. Closer still, some of Ceres town harbour was also visible. At the bottom of the hill beyond the terrace where they were now sitting was the small bay where she and Demetrius had occasionally swum. Not often, because they'd thought it safer to walk over the hills to one of the quieter bays where they wouldn't be seen.

She pointed at the hillside that skirted the bay. 'There's Michaelis's house. Sara is so happy there.'

'Is Sara going to stop working after she gets married? She's a good staff nurse. We'd miss her in the emergency department.'

'She told me yesterday she would continue working until the babies came along,' Chloe said. 'That's what I planned to do before I knew the babies were on their way.'

'You said Patrick died when the twins were only three months old,' Demetrius said quietly. 'That must have been traumatic for you.'

Chloe hesitated as she remembered that awful day when the police had arrived at the house.

'Yes, it was. Patrick had been driving his parents home after an evening with us. He was driving down the motorway. A huge lorry went out of control and broke through the crash barrier. Patrick's car was crushed underneath it. The lorry driver suffered minor injuries. Patrick died at the scene of the crash and his parents shortly afterwards in hospital.'

She took a sip of her drink. She'd recited this story so often but it still affected her. She was still overcome by the mixture of grief and horror.

'Oh, Demetrius!' Chloe put down her glass on the wooden table and covered her face with her hands. 'Patrick didn't deserve to—'

Demetrius put his arms round her and drew her against him.

'Shh! Life is never fair, Chloe. It would have been so much better for everybody if you hadn't gone back to him. I could never understand why you—'

'But you told me to go back!' Chloe blinked away the tears and turned her blazingly furious eyes on Demetrius. 'If you'd wanted me to stay I would have stayed but you didn't!'

Demetrius was looking perplexed. 'I told you to go back?' he repeated quietly. 'When did I ever...?'

'In your letter.'

'What letter?'

'The letter you sent me the day I was supposed to meet

you. You must remember! I can remember every detail of it even though I tore it up and threw it away so I would never have to read it again. I couldn't bear to keep it as a permanent reminder of how you rejected me.'

'I didn't send you a letter, Chloe.' Demetrius's voice was ominously calm and quiet.

'You gave it to Vanessa. She brought it straight over from your house, she told me.'

'Vanessa?'

'The woman we saw today down in the harbour. I was friendly with her that summer. Her father has that big house built at the side of the bay down there. We all thought it was going to be a hotel until we realised it was a luxurious family home. Vanessa's family used to come to the house for part of the summer, but in the winter months it stood empty. Now, apparently, it's going to be sold.'

As Chloe pointed down the hillside she could feel her pulses racing. For the first time in eight years she had reason to doubt what had happened. Although she'd totally trusted her helpful friend during that summer, she was beginning to wonder if her trust had been misplaced.

'Vanessa was a good friend to me that summer,' Chloe said, trying desperately to make sense of what had happened. 'I can't believe she would want to deceive me. After we'd made friends I used her as an excuse to come over and meet you. Don't you remember?'

'Oh, yes, I remember.' Demetrius said evenly. 'Tell me exactly what happened when Vanessa brought you a letter.'

Chloe took a sip of her drink. 'Well, you remember the day before I was due to go back to England?'

'How could I forget it! I remember we arranged to meet during the morning down there in the bay. You arrived in a dreadful state, worrying about how you were going to break the news to your parents that you weren't going to get back with Patrick, that you'd met someone here on the island and you were going to stay here.'

Demetrius cleared his throat. 'I remember suggesting that you go away and make sure that you were doing the right thing. I asked you to come to the house that evening but you said your parents were expecting you to stay in for a farewell dinner party. You said you would try to come to the taverna at the beginning of Nimborio Bay.'

Demetrius's expression was deadly serious. 'I said that if you didn't come, it would mean you'd decided to go back to England. You also gave me the impression that you had no intention of going back. That you were going to tell your parents that you were staying on the island, before meeting me at the taverna.'

'Demetrius, believe me, as I walked back over the hill into the town, that was exactly what I'd intended to do. And that was when I met Vanessa. She'd been down by the waterside. You remember we often used to see her there and she liked to chat to someone her own age. If she was going shopping she would walk back over the hill with me, like she did on that occasion.'

'Did Vanessa know we were together?'

Chloe hesitated. 'Demetrius, she was the only person on the island who knew. I was so relieved to be able to confide in someone. She was the sort of girl who seemed so utterly trustworthy. Soon after we met she said she'd seen you and me together from the house and we seemed very much in love. I was only twenty. I needed somebody to confide in.'

'So you told her about us?'

'Yes, I told her. And I also told her about Patrick.'

Chloe felt a tremor of apprehension run through her as she saw Demetrius's disapproving expression.

'I know I should have kept quiet, but... Anyway, on my last day on Ceres, after I'd said goodbye to you, Vanessa came hurrying after me as I walked over the hill. She said she'd noticed us talking and it looked very serious this time. I told her I had to make sure I made the right decision. I explained that if I didn't turn up at the taverna to meet you, that would mean that I was going back to England, and if I did...'

'So Vanessa knew all about the meeting we'd set up,' Demetrius said.

'Yes, she did. She told me she hoped I was going to stay on the island, that she would miss me if I went back. I told her I'd already decided to stay and I was going to tell you that evening. During the afternoon I was walking along the beach in front of our house, planning what I was going to say to Patrick. How I was going to soften the blow. How I was going to break the news to the family. Suddenly I saw a boat speeding across the water towards me.'

Demetrius frowned. 'Vanessa! Was it that flash speedboat belonging to her father? The one where she invited us on board for drinks one afternoon when her father was away on business?'

Chloe nodded. 'Yes, it was. She had that young man who used to work for their family steering it across the water at a tremendous pace. I thought it must be something urgent. She leapt off the boat, I remember, looking dreadfully anxious, and handed me your letter.'

'Chloe, I never sent you a letter!'

'Well, Vanessa said it was from you. I'd never had a letter from you before, never even seen your handwriting, so I had no reason to doubt it was from you. It was typewritten. You'd once told me you always typed your letters because your handwriting was becoming indecipherable, like a typical doctor's. But there was a scrawled signature in ink at the end. It looked vaguely like your name.'

'What did the letter say?'

'So you really don't know, do you?'

'Of course I don't know!'

'In your letter…in this letter, it said you'd come to the conclusion that I ought to go back to England. You wanted me to forget you. Our affair had been a mistake. You wished you'd never got involved with me because it could only lead to trouble and you had to concentrate on your medical career. I was too much of a distraction for you and…oh, it went on and on, convincing me that we had no future together.'

Demetrius remained silent as she finished speaking. After several seconds had elapsed he spoke in a calm but weary voice.

'And you believed I would send you a letter like that? After all we'd meant to each other?'

'I had no reason to doubt it. It seems strange now but I was prepared to believe that you'd had a complete change of heart. But if you didn't write the letter then who did?'

'Vanessa,' Demetrius said grimly.

'Oh, no! Vanessa was my friend. I trusted her. I—'

'Then your trust was misplaced. I never really liked the girl. I always suspected she could be two-faced.' Demetrius hesitated. 'Soon after you'd gone back to England she came to the house one evening—uninvited, of course. Said she'd heard you'd left me and she thought I might need some company.'

'Well, that's the sort of girl she was. She liked to be helpful.'

'Chloe, Vanessa wasn't trying to be helpful. She made

it quite plain she wanted to step into your shoes. I made it clear that I wasn't interested in her. But she kept pestering me, following me. She was obsessed with the idea that she could wear me down until I took her on as my girlfriend.'

'So that's why she wanted to get me out of the way.'

'Got it in one! And not only did I have to keep pushing her away, I was missing you so much.'

'Were you missing me?'

'Of course I was missing you. Chloe, I found it hard to concentrate on my work at the hospital. And then that dreadful girl phoning me up, just happening to be in the taverna where I'd gone for a drink. Just happening to be in the upper town and deciding to call in and see how I was getting along. In the end I realised I had to get away from the island. Have a complete change of scene.'

'So that was when you decided to go to Australia.'

'There was a hospital in Sydney advertising in one of the medical journals for medical staff. I applied and was accepted for interview. I resigned from Ceres hospital and flew to Australia. If they hadn't taken me I would have had to keep trying till I found work. But at least I wasn't reminded of you every time I came back into this house.'

'Oh, Demetrius. It could have been so different, couldn't it?'

Chloe wanted so much to believe that Demetrius was telling her the truth about the letter and being totally honest about the part that Vanessa had played in his life.

'We've wasted so much time.' Demetrius stood up, taking both her hands in his, drawing her to her feet.

She moulded herself against his hard body, feeling the hardening of his desire matching her own sensual arousal. They only had to make the slightest physical contact with each other and their bodies reacted as if by one and the same passionate stimulus.

'Let's go to bed,' he whispered.

'Mmm…'

She was too happy for words as Demetrius carried her up the ancient wooden staircase to the cosy, low-ceilinged bedroom at the top of the house.

As he laid her down on the antique white embroidered coverlet she couldn't believe that she was once more in this room where they'd spent so many idyllic hours. Their own secret love nest! It was like a heavenly dream come true. The intrinsic scent of the old house enveloped her. Centuries of happy couples must have made love in this room. The ambience of simplicity oozed romance. Babies had been conceived here, babies had probably been born here. And this was where she belonged, in Demetrius's arms…

The moon was peeping through the small window that looked out towards the hillside sloping down to the bay. Chloe stirred in Demetrius's arms, wondering how long she'd been asleep. By the light of the moon she could just make out the hands of the bedside clock. Too long! She ought to get back home.

She tried to extricate herself from the sleeping Demetrius's arms but he simply held her closer, murmuring softly as he opened his eyes and smiled at her.

'I've got to go home, Demetrius.'

'Why?' Demetrius was wide awake now. 'You're a twenty-eight-year-old woman. The twins are away for the night so you can please yourself. You've phoned your mother, told her you'll be late. Isn't it time you cut the apron strings?'

'Demetrius,' she said, moving involuntarily further

away from him, 'I have a commitment to my family. My parents were very supportive to me when I was left alone to bring up two babies.'

Demetrius rolled onto his side and looked at her with an intense expression. 'My babies,' he said evenly. 'You could have contacted me.'

'I thought about it,' she said. 'Believe me, I was so often on the point of trying to find you…but I thought you didn't want me. And later on I heard you were in Australia and I expected you would have married and probably started a family of your own. An old flame announcing she'd given birth to your twins wouldn't have been exactly welcomed.'

'How did you know I'd gone to Australia, Chloe?'

'I came out to Ceres with my parents when the twins were three years old. My father was planning to retire and negotiating to buy the house at that point. I intended to stay only one week—'

'One week! Why?'

'I simply wanted to find out what had happened to you. When I heard you were living permanently in Australia I knew it would be safe for me to stay longer.'

'Safe?'

Demetrius's voice sounded very hard. Chloe held out her arms towards him as she moved nearer. 'Don't let's quarrel, Demetrius. It's been so wonderful to be with you again.'

He smiled as he drew her against his hard body. 'I don't want us to quarrel either. Not here in this bed where we made love so often before you went away.'

Chloe leaned her head against Demetrius's shoulder as the memories flooded back.

'That night you brought me home, only a week after I met you, it was my first time, Demetrius,' she said softly.

'I remember,' Demetrius murmured. 'And I remember I was so worried afterwards that you might be upset at losing your virginity. But you reassured me, told me that you'd wanted it this way.'

'I was so much in love with you.'

'And I knew I wanted to spend the rest of my life with you,' Demetrius said softly.

'I think it's called destiny,' Chloe said, her voice betraying the strong emotion she was feeling.

'Chloe, the sooner you tear yourself away from your parents and acknowledge your real family...'

'What are you saying, Demetrius?'

'I'm saying that I want you to come and live with me here where you belong. Bring our daughters and we'll start a new life as a real family. Chloe, my darling, will you marry me?'

Chloe looked into Demetrius's dark, expressive eyes and felt as if her heart would burst with happiness. But at the same time...

'Demetrius, I can't give you an answer yet. I want to stay in my family home until after Sara's wedding. I'm not free to leave just yet. They all need me to give support and—'

Demetrius gave a sigh of exasperation. 'I know, I know.' He pulled a wry face. 'You need more time to think, just like last time...'

'But it's not like last time!' Chloe said. 'Last time I didn't know you wanted me.'

Demetrius reached forward and drew her into the circle of his arms. 'Of course I wanted you.'

She hesitated. 'Tell me about your marriage. Why did it fail?'

Demetrius leaned back against the pillows. 'Debora and I simply didn't have enough in common, apart from the fact that we were both doctors—that was about the sum of it. I met her soon after I flew to Sydney and joined the medical staff of the hospital. Debora was English, I was Greek. We were both lonely expatriates, both involved in our work at the hospital and very little else. I asked her out a couple of times. She suggested I move into her apartment.'

'Did you love her?'

'Not at that point. It was simply convenient for both of us to have a base together. Little by little I became fond of her and it seemed logical to get married. We flew to Bali and got married on the beach.'

'Sounds romantic!'

'Not really! It was convenient. We both took a week off from the hospital. As soon as we got back, we both became more involved with our work again. Our personal life became non-existent. I found myself hoping that my off-duty time wouldn't coincide with Debora's. When I found out she was having an affair it was almost a relief. Our divorce was perfectly amicable.'

'We've both made mistakes, haven't we, Demetrius? We both know what it's like to be with the wrong person.'

Demetrius tightened his arms around her. 'I know what it's like to be with someone I really love as well. That's the most wonderful thing in the world.'

He kissed her with a tender gentleness that ignited the strong desire stirring within her. As his kiss deepened Chloe could feel her body turning into liquid fire. The touch of his fingers on her skin and his ardent caresses were driving her wild with renewed desire for a confirmation of their unquenchable love for each other.

As he entered her she moaned with delight, revelling in the sensation of his strong manhood thrusting deeper and deeper inside her. And at the moment of earth-shattering climax, she cried out in ecstasy...

It was daylight when she awoke. She'd stirred once as the dawn had been breaking over the window-sill, but had decided that she couldn't leave the house yet. Closing her eyes and snuggling closer to Demetrius, she'd decided that she may as well be hung for a sheep as a lamb.

Tiptoeing out of bed so as not to waken Demetrius, she went down to the little bathroom with the quaint old bath. It was more of a hip bath than a full-size bath, but she was able to squeeze herself in and lie back as the steamy water poured in. The narrow pipes were making loud clanking noises as the water started to flow.

She smiled to herself as she lay back. The plumbing system on this island was intensely complicated and hopelessly but endearingly inefficient. Demetrius had told her that the water system in the house had been added by his father with the help of a man who'd claimed to be a plumber. When the house had been built about five hundred years ago, there had been no plumbing, of course. And so it had remained for centuries.

But there was nothing she would like better than to move into this lovely old house. Once she had sorted out the complications of how she was going to break away from one family unit and explain to the girls that they were actually part of another...

'There you are, Chloe!' Demetrius stood in the doorway. 'I woke up and you weren't there. I thought you'd left me until I heard the water pipes clanking.'

Chloe smiled. 'I'm trying to gather my thoughts. Get ready for going back to reality. I'm not sure what kind of a reception I'll get at home.'

'Does it matter?'

'It does to me,' she said quietly.

'Ring them now. Say you'll pick up the twins from the house where they've spent the night and take them to school before you go to the hospital.'

Demetrius was kneeling beside the bath, taking her face in his hands, looking at her with that appealing expression that could melt all her resolve.

'All right, I will,' she said.

'Good luck!'

Demetrius stood up and handed her a large fluffy towel. As she stepped out of the bath, he enveloped her in it, holding her close.

'I'll get my mobile,' she said quickly, before she could change her mind. 'I'll say I'll pick up the twins but I won't talk about the fact that—'

Demetrius sighed. 'You don't want to upset your mother, do you?'

'Not yet. Later, when the time is right... Oh, hello, Mum, yes, I'm fine...'

CHAPTER SEVEN

CHLOE glanced out of the window of her office. The harbour looked even busier than usual. Small boats coming and going, a larger pleasure boat setting off for a trip around the island with a stop for a barbecue lunch and some swimming in a quiet, picturesque bay. There were tourists wandering along the waterside, local people hurrying between the shops, filling their baskets with provisions.

August was the height of the summer holidays for the tourists and the busiest time of the year for the hospital. Michaelis had told her last month that he was advertising for more medical staff, both doctors and nurses.

As Chloe sat down at her desk to attend to some of the paperwork, she reflected that time was passing very quickly. She was glad to have reached August without rocking the family boat too much! At the end of this month Michaelis and Sara would marry and she would be free of her obligations at home. She would then have to explain everything about her complicated relationship with Demetrius to her mother.

'I did knock but you were miles away!' Demetrius was standing beside her desk.

Chloe pushed her papers to one side. 'I was trying to focus my thoughts on this report the police sent. Michaelis wants me to write up exactly what happened the day that Vasilio was snatched from the nursery. It's almost a month since it happened so I'm having to refer to the notes I made in my ward report. Time passes so quickly.'

'Thank goodness!' Demetrius said with heartfelt feeling. 'How are Sara's wedding plans going?'

Chloe groaned. 'Don't ask! Mum's in a permanent state of anxiety. I'll be glad when it's all over.'

'So will I,' Demetrius said meaningfully.

For a moment Chloe thought Demetrius was going to question her as to whether she'd thought out how she was going to break away from her family after the wedding. She'd noticed that since that wonderful night together he'd been careful not to bring up the matter, and for that she was truly grateful.

He hadn't even asked her over to his house again. It was as if, like her, he was living in a state of limbo, holding his emotions in check, not daring to look too far ahead.

A couple of times they'd gone out for a meal in a taverna, but after driving her home Demetrius had left immediately.

'How are Rachel and Samantha?' Demetrius asked.

'They're very well.' Chloe looked up at Demetrius, her eyes full of sympathy as she saw the hauntingly anxious expression on his face. 'Their snorkelling is coming on tremendously well. We swim most evenings when I'm off duty and see the most amazing fish in the bay in front of the house.'

They were his daughters. He often asked about them and she knew he longed to see them again. And she felt so torn between her loyalty to the family who'd sustained her through the early years of the twins' lives and the man who was their father.

'They're taking part in the Ceres Music Festival in a week's time,' she said quickly, watching as Demetrius's intense interest in his daughters showed in his expression. 'Stavros, the music director of the festival, has written a musical for children based on the story of Demeter and her daughter Persephone.'

Demetrius nodded. 'Yes, I heard about it from Sara when I was working with her in the emergency department last week.'

Chloe smiled. 'Sara's heavily involved in the organisation of the festival and the training of the children. That's another distraction for her at this busy time before her wedding. But she promised to help Stavros before the date for the wedding was set.'

'Michaelis told me that Sara graduated from music college before doing her nursing training,' Demetrius said. 'A talented girl, your sister.'

Chloe smiled. 'Yes, we're all very proud of her. Rachel and Samantha think she's wonderful when she coaches them in their singing. They're only in the chorus. The main parts are being taken by the older children. But there's a lot to learn and they're thoroughly enjoying themselves.'

'I'd like to watch the performance,' Demetrius said evenly.

'Of course!' Chloe spoke quickly, endorsing the idea with a confidence she didn't feel.

She knew how much Rachel and Samantha would love to see Demetrius but the possibility of a showdown between Demetrius and her mother would spoil the day.

Demetrius's eyes remained cool and enigmatic. 'Sara tells me the children's musical is being staged in one of the bays further down the coast. They're building a stage, seats for the spectators and a barbecue area.'

'It's going to be a wonderful event.' Chloe raised her eyes to Demetrius's. 'We mustn't spoil it by doing anything that would—'

'I'll pretend I don't know what you mean,' he said quietly, picking up the police report from Chloe's desk as if anxious to change the subject. 'Michaelis gave me a copy of this but I haven't had time to study it yet. Such a tragedy, wasn't it?'

Demetrius put the report back on Chloe's desk.

Chloe nodded as she glanced over the sheaf of papers. 'Apparently, Diana's mother was English and her father Greek. She lives on Rhodes. It was all so sad. She'd recently lost her own baby. Her husband desperately wants a family and she was pinning her hopes on a child to save her marriage. When their baby died, she confided in her friend who agreed to help her find another baby.'

'That was the blonde woman, wasn't it?'

Chloe nodded. 'She even got her children to help. They didn't know what it was all about, of course. Diana applied for a job as a temporary receptionist at the hospital. She had good references and was taken on immediately as we're short-staffed at the moment.'

'But the irony of the situation is that Diana's husband is standing by her now, defending what she did. It appears her marriage wasn't as rocky as she'd thought.'

Chloe switched on her computer. 'I think the poor girl is having therapy. She needs to be pitied more than condemned. All I've got to do now is fill in what happened here at the hospital.'

'Will you have time to do some real nursing later this morning?'

'I hope so! What did you have in mind?'

'We've got to come to a decision about how we're going to treat Fiona.'

'I hadn't forgotten. I've put Fiona down on the theatre list for later this morning,' Chloe said as she turned away from the computer and focussed her mind on their placental abruption patient. 'I'd made a note in the diary about her. The pregnancy is now thirty-eight weeks.'

'I'd always hoped Fiona would stick it out until the

thirty-eighth week. We're lucky not to have had to intervene before, aren't we?'

'The foetus was strong and healthy when I did the last scan, but Fiona's getting more and more impatient. The last few weeks have been a testing time for her. I've booked the theatre for eleven o'clock. Michaelis was going to ask you to do the examination and deliver the baby, using whatever method you decided was appropriate.'

'Yes, Michaelis came to see me about Fiona's case, but he didn't discuss nursing staff. I'd like you to be there to assist me, Chloe. You're the one who's most helped Fiona through this difficult time and I think she'd be more confident if she knew you were in Theatre.'

'Fine!' Chloe said briskly. 'I'll see you in a couple of hours, then.'

Demetrius paused at the door. 'You look so sexy when you're in your efficient mood.'

Chloe smiled, trying hard to keep her eyes focussed on her computer report. Working with Demetrius was a disturbing but infinitely rewarding experience. Oh, how she longed to have all the secrets out in the open! Soon she would be able to. But she was still desperately apprehensive of the new problems that would arrive when the revelations were made.

Forcing herself into professional mode, she finished the report as quickly as possible, printed it out and asked a junior nurse to take it to Michaelis's office. Now she was able to continue with the work she enjoyed the most. Real hands-on nursing!

She did a round of her patients, giving each one as much time as she could spare, noting their problems, checking their medication, their general health and the social situation they would return to when they were discharged.

Leaving Fiona as her last patient, Chloe spent several

minutes explaining what was going to happen. She'd already briefed her patient earlier that morning, checking that she hadn't had anything to eat since midnight.

'We're going to take you along to Theatre about eleven o'clock, Fiona,' Chloe said in a reassuring voice. 'Dr Demetrius will examine you internally. If he's satisfied there is no further abnormality, we'll assist you to go into labour and you'll give birth naturally.'

'And what if there is something abnormal?' Fiona asked quietly.

'Well, as you know, there was a problem with the placenta after your car crash. If the situation has worsened, it would be advisable for us to deliver Tommy by Caesarean section. That's why you've had nothing to eat or drink since last night, just in case you need a general anaesthetic. You've already signed a consent form agreeing that if this is necessary you—'

'Yes, yes,' Fiona said quickly. 'Whatever needs doing, I know you'll see to it. You and Dr Demetrius have been great! You will be there in Theatre, won't you, Chloe? I asked Demetrius to make sure you would be.'

Chloe smiled. 'Demetrius passed on your message, Fiona.'

Fiona patted her tummy. 'Did you hear that, Tommy? You'd better put that football away and start getting yourself ready to make an entrance. Put your best football shirt on, darling.'

Chloe squeezed her patient's hand before moving away. All through the weeks of waiting Fiona had tried to stay positive but Chloe knew how apprehensive she really was. Chloe prayed silently that all would go well.

Demetrius peeled off his sterile gloves and handed them to a junior nurse who threw them in the bin at the back of the operating theatre. For a few moments Demetrius considered the situation. The blood accumulating in his patient's womb and vagina pointed to a worsening of the placental abruption. After checking the ultrasound scan performed just before the operation, Demetrius had taken the precaution of anaesthetising Fiona before he'd started his examination.

He glanced across the operating table to Chloe. 'We'll need to get this baby out by Caesarean section,' he said quietly. 'You explained the implications to Fiona, didn't you, Chloe?'

Chloe could see the anxious expression in the eyes above the mask. She nodded. 'Fiona is prepared for all eventualities.'

Demetrius left the table briefly to scrub up again, change his theatre clothes and put on another pair of sterile gloves. The anaesthetist was checking the cylinders at the head of the operating table. Chloe waited, hoping against hope that they wouldn't find any further abnormalities. She'd cherished this patient and her unborn child for so long now that she felt personally responsible for her well-being.

Demetrius was back in his place again, across the table from her, looking calm and confident.

'Scalpel, please.'

Chloe picked up the scalpel and watched as Demetrius made the first incision. Carefully and with great precision, Demetrius cut through the abdominal wall before making an incision in the lower segment of the womb. In a matter of minutes he was lifting out the small baby, holding him high above the mother so that the assembled theatre team could admire the perfectly formed infant.

As she listened to the squalling baby complaining bitterly about being lifted out of his cosy nest, Chloe had to blink back tears of happiness. Demetrius was smiling as he handed the messy little bundle across the table.

'There you go, Chloe. Usual checks, please. I'll perform the final embroidery and make sure that Fiona can wear a bikini again.'

'So this is my Tommy!' Fiona smiled groggily as she held out her arms to take her baby for the first time. 'He's beautiful—but a bit small.'

'That was the only size we had in the shop today, madam. He's big enough,' Chloe said, feeling relieved that Fiona had eventually come round from the anaesthetic OK.

It had taken longer than usual for Fiona to open her eyes and Chloe had actually paged the anaesthetist only minutes before. They were still in the antetheatre. Chloe was aware that she should get back to the ward but she was unwilling to leave her patient to the theatre staff. She felt personally responsible for this special patient and wanted to see the operation through to a successful conclusion.

The swing doors opened and Demetrius came in, pulling off his green theatre cap and loosening his mask. A nurse was unfastening the Velcro strips at the back of his gown.

'Our anaesthetist will be with you in a couple of minutes, Chloe. What's the problem?'

Chloe smiled. 'Problem solved.' She lowered her voice. 'I thought Fiona was taking too long to come round.'

'You worry too much,' Demetrius said quietly, resting his arm on her shoulder for a few moments as he looked down at her with quizzical eyes. 'You shouldn't take on all the cares of the world.'

Chloe revelled in the tender tone of Demetrius's voice but he changed swiftly back into his professional self as he turned to speak to their patient.

'So how are you feeling, Fiona?'

Fiona gave a strained grin. 'Like a ten-ton elephant has just walked over my tummy. But it was all worth it just to get my Tommy out. He's already crying because he can't find his football. He must have left it behind.'

'Let me take him now, Fiona,' Chloe said, reaching forward. 'You're going to need a lot of rest so we're going to put Tommy in the nursery.'

'Are you sure he'll be safe in the nursery, Sister?' Fiona asked anxiously. 'I mean, only last month, that baby…'

'Don't worry, Fiona,' Demetrius said reassuringly. 'After the police did their full-scale investigation of the hospital, we've made a lot of changes. We've had extra security people appointed and precautions implemented since that baby was taken away. It couldn't happen again.'

He turned to look at Chloe. 'Thanks, Chloe. Mother and baby can go back to the ward now.'

It had been a busy afternoon. Fiona wasn't Chloe's only post-operative patient. Being in charge of the whole of the floor, Chloe had spent her time checking out other patients in the gynaecological and general surgical wards. Each ward had a trained nurse in charge but it was Chloe who had ultimate responsibility.

Sitting at her desk now, finishing off her report, she realised she was feeling more tired than usual. She signed her name at the bottom of the page before putting down her pen and leaning back against her chair. What she needed was some real relaxation.

As the door opened she smiled. It was almost as if her wish had come true. The only true way she ever relaxed was when she was with Demetrius. Looking at him now, striding over to her desk, she wondered what it would be like when she was able to bring the truth out into the open. They'd both been so careful at the hospital to keep their

relationship secret. And off duty, they'd tried not to be
seen together in compromising situations. But the strain of
keeping up this charade was beginning to tell. This was
what was tiring her more than any stress she might feel in
her work at the hospital. She'd been trained to cope with
responsibility, with medical emergencies. But she hadn't
been trained to cope with endless secrecy, duplicity,
guilt...

'What's the problem?' Demetrius leaned over her desk
and touched the side of her face. 'You look like the cares
of the world are all on your shoulders.'

'That's how I feel.'

'Then let me take you away from all this. What time do
you go off duty?'

'In about half an hour, when I've given the report. But,
Demetrius, I want to go home to Rachel and Samantha.'

'There could be a solution to that,' he said gravely. 'I
could take you and the girls out this evening. All you have
to do is—'

'Demetrius, we've been over that ground before. At the
end of the month, as soon as Sara and Michaelis are safely
married, I'll tell my family about us.'

'I want to be with you when you make the announcement, Chloe.'

'Thanks, Demetrius, I'd like your support.'

'Oh, well, if you won't let me take you and the girls
out this evening, I'll settle for a quick drink before I drive
you home. Phone Manolis and tell him you're getting a
lift home so you don't need him to collect you in the boat.'

Chloe was feeling more relaxed already. Just to be with
Demetrius for a few minutes would ease the tension.

'You can be so persuasive, Demetrius.'

'But not persuasive enough to make you see that there's

no need for all this pretence to carry on any longer. If only you would—'

'Please, Demetrius. We agreed, didn't we?'

Demetrius gave a sigh of resignation. 'See you in half an hour, OK? In the car park. I know you don't like to be seen leaving with me from Reception. Somebody might jump to conclusions.'

She watched him going towards the door. His tone had been harsh and impatient. She longed to hurry after him, tell him she wanted to shout their news to the whole world, but she forced herself to remain absolutely still.

Demetrius changed down a gear as they descended the steep winding road that led to the bay below his house. Chloe had agreed that the waterside taverna where they used to meet would be the safest place for their quick drink. This was a quiet part of Ceres, frequented rarely by the medical staff of the hospital. They could just as easily have gone to Demetrius's home for a drink but Chloe knew what would have happened if they'd been alone in the house.

There wasn't time! She'd promised not to be late this evening.

As they got out of the car in front of the taverna, Chloe glanced up at the large imposing house overlooking the bay.

'I see Vanessa's house is still up for sale.'

Chloe still had mixed feelings about the girl who had supposedly betrayed her trust and caused her to change the whole course of her life. She still couldn't believe it had happened. Vanessa had seemed so utterly genuine in her friendship. Had she been plotting to take Demetrius away from her all the time that they'd been friends?

'Yes, I noticed it when I came down here the other day.

You've lived on the island longer than me more recently—
how long has it been for sale, Chloe?'

'It's been boarded up for the last couple of years. Nobody used it. And then early this year the sign appeared.
Vanessa's father must have finally decided it's not worth
keeping on if nobody in the family wants to use it.'

She followed Demetrius between the tables that had
been set out along the narrow strip of land that jutted out
into the sea in front of the taverna. They were the only
people there. Demetrius chose the table nearest the sea.

'I'm glad our favourite table is still here,' Chloe said,
leaning from her chair to dip her hand in the water.

She could hear Demetrius ordering their drinks. They
always had glasses of ouzo here with a carafe of water and
a plate of olives and feta cheese.

A shoal of tiny fish was swimming nearby. She picked
up a piece of bread from the basket already set out on the
table and held it in her hand. One of the fish, more ad-
venturous than the rest, swam up and nibbled at the bread
between her fingers.

Chloe laughed. 'Oh, this fish is tickling me!'

Demetrius leaned across the table. 'It's good to hear you
laugh again, Chloe,' he said. 'You've been so tense in
recent weeks. I'm longing to make you happy again.'

Chloe swallowed. 'I am happy, Demetrius. Just finding
you again, knowing that it was all a mistake, that…'

A shadow had fallen across the table. Someone was
standing between the sea and the rays of the setting sun.

'Hello, Chloe, I've been wondering when we'd meet
again.'

Chloe looked up as she heard the unmistakable voice,
recognised that long auburn, glossy hair, the impeccably
manicured, crimson-painted nails.

'Vanessa!'

'I've been going to call you, Chloe, but I just never got around to it. May I sit down?'

'I don't think that would be a good idea, do you, Vanessa?' Demetrius said, his voice steely calm.

Chloe watched as Vanessa's face turned bright red.

'I can see I'm not wanted, so...' Vanessa shrugged. 'Bye!'

Chloe watched Vanessa leisurely sauntering away between the tables that were now beginning to fill up with tourists. The encounter had been so brief! She'd wanted to ask so many questions.

'Demetrius, did you have to be so rude?'

Demetrius frowned. 'I didn't want Vanessa to be here at the same table with us. After all that's happened!'

'But that's the whole point! We don't know what happened. We've only surmised that it was Vanessa who wrote that letter. We need to ask her outright if—'

'And do you think she'd tell us the truth?'

Chloe sighed in exasperation. 'I don't know, but we could have asked her. At least—'

'And spoil our few precious minutes together?'

Chloe stared across the table at Demetrius. Seeing the angry expression on his face, she realised that she didn't know him as well as she'd thought she did. She'd never known Demetrius behave like this before and she took exception to his attitude.

'Don't you think our precious minutes have been spoiled already, Demetrius?' she asked evenly.

Pushing back her chair, she stood up. Yes, she would show Demetrius that she was angry, too. She didn't like the man she'd seen revealed just now. This wasn't the man she'd fallen in love with, and she didn't like the disturbing thoughts that were coming into her head.

Demetrius stood up. 'I'll take you home,' he said, tight-lipped as he picked up the car keys from the table.

Neither of them spoke on the drive over to Nimborio. Chloe stared out of the window. Why hadn't Demetrius allowed her the opportunity of asking Vanessa why she'd delivered that letter…unless…?

She couldn't help wondering if Demetrius had secrets he was afraid Vanessa would reveal. Had he been telling the truth when he'd said that Vanessa had chased him and he'd refused to have anything to do with her?

Was that the real truth or could Vanessa have made some unwanted revelations? Vanessa was a very attractive woman. Perhaps Demetrius hadn't discouraged her advances. Perhaps…

Chloe swallowed hard, hoping against hope that she was wrong in her suppositions. She had to give Demetrius the benefit of the doubt, but looking at him now, frowning as he drove the car furiously around the narrow road that skirted the bay, she found it very hard to make an objective judgement.

Demetrius pulled up in front of the house, scattering a hail of gravel behind him as he braked. She began to open the door, but Demetrius had already jumped down and was coming round to help her out.

Ever the gentleman, even when he was angry with her. She averted her eyes as he held out his arms to help her down the steep step to the ground. She didn't want to have to witness the angry look on his face. She didn't want to remember that hostile expression in the small hours of the night when she was sure she would be lying awake, worrying about how this was all going to end.

Demetrius moved away from her, walking quickly around the front of the car. His hand was on the door as he prepared to haul himself back into the driver's seat.

'Demetrius! I can't let you go like this!'

He raised an eyebrow. 'Like what?'

'I don't like us to quarrel.' She moved closer. 'But I have to know the truth. Seeing Vanessa this evening, it brought it all back to me. The letter…do you really think Vanessa wrote it? Or…I have to ask you this…was your relationship with Vanessa platonic, or—?'

Demetrius climbed into the car and started the engine. Leaning out of the window, he called to her, 'I don't think that question dignifies an answer. Goodbye, Chloe.'

'Demetrius, wait!'

Demetrius was already speeding off down the road.

'Mummy, Mummy!' The twins were hurrying down the path from the house.

'Mummy, that was Demetrius, wasn't it?' Samantha shouted.

'Why didn't you ask him in?' Rachel looked furiously indignant. 'You told us he was always too busy to come round but he can't be busy tonight. And we haven't seen him for ages. Did you ask Demetrius if he would come to see us singing in the festival?'

Chloe knelt down, taking comfort from the little arms around her neck. 'Demetrius said he would try to go to the festival,' she began haltingly.

It seemed such a long time since she and Demetrius had spoken about it. She hadn't envisaged they would have a full-scale row this evening. She'd never thought that the wonderful ambience that had existed between them could be shattered like this.

'Goody!' Rachel smiled happily. 'I'm glad he's coming.'

'Demetrius only said he would try to be there,' Chloe stressed. 'If he's too busy at the hospital then—'

'I hope he does come,' Samantha said quietly. 'Don't you, Mum?'

Chloe nodded, her heart too full for words as she watched Demetrius's car disappear around the bend that led back to Ceres town. When she finally managed to speak, her voice was quivering with emotion.

'Yes, I hope Demetrius will be there, but we can't be certain he will be. And if he's not, you mustn't be too disappointed.'

CHAPTER EIGHT

SITTING in the prow of the fishing boat, feeling the sea breeze ruffling her hair, Chloe knew she should be enjoying herself, along with all the other people who were going to the music festival. But the last week had seemed the longest in her life! Working with Demetrius at the hospital had been torture. He'd treated her like a distant acquaintance who simply happened to be a medical colleague.

'Would you and the girls like a drink, Chloe?'

Chloe looked up and smiled at her sister. Sara was precariously holding onto a tray of drinks as the boat, rocking from side to side, pursued its course through the gentle waves.

'There's fruit juice, ouzo, retsina…'

'Fruit juice, please, Sara, for all of us.'

Her sister moved on to serve more drinks. Looking out across the water, Chloe could see several boats speeding alongside. Every available craft seemed to have been called into action today to transport the children and their parents to the picturesque uninhabited bay where the musical was to be performed as part of the festival. The children were all excitedly chattering about what was going to happen, if they could remember their lines, what they were going to have for the barbecue lunch.

Chloe took a sip of her drink and looked down at Rachel, curled up on a pile of ropes beside her. Her daughter's eyes were closed and her face was set in a frown.

'Are you all right, Rachel?'

'I've got a headache, Mum.'

'I'm not surprised with all this noise going on. I'll get somebody to turn the music down.'

'It doesn't matter,' Rachel said listlessly.

'Are you going to have your drink?'

Rachel closed her eyes more tightly. 'No, thanks.'

Automatically, Chloe reached across and put her fingers over her daughter's wrist to check her pulse. It wasn't like Rachel to be so quiet. Maybe she was sickening for something.

Rachel's pulse was a bit quicker than usual, but Chloe reasoned that it could be all the excitement. Her skin felt unusually hot, too. She wasn't going to start searching for a thermometer in the first-aid box. Not at this stage anyway. She would wait and see what developed.

'You don't have to sing in the chorus if you're not feeling well, darling,' she whispered.

'I want to sing!'

Chloe felt relieved as Rachel displayed some of her usual sparky character. Perhaps she was worrying too much about her daughter. Maybe it was because she herself hadn't had enough sleep this week.

She looked out across the water again, shielding her eyes against the strong morning sun. A cream and yellow speedboat was about to pass them. The fishing boat in which she was being transported would feel the wash caused by the more powerful boat if their captain didn't take evasive action.

Chloe could see a Greek man at the controls of the speedboat. Where had she seen him before? And there were several passengers enjoying themselves at the back of the boat where drinks were being served.

She started in surprise as she recognised one of the passengers...no, two of the passengers, sitting near each other. Demetrius and Vanessa! She couldn't see the expressions on their faces as they were too far away, but it didn't look as if Demetrius was objecting to spending time with the woman who'd wreaked such havoc in their lives.

Chloe felt a chilling anger rising up inside her, followed by a deep-seated feeling of despair. She turned away and looked down the length of the boat, trying to concentrate on the day ahead, willing herself to join in the general carnival atmosphere.

But it was impossible when you felt as if your own world was falling apart. All the hopes and dreams that had been with her since Demetrius had come back into her life were crumbling around her.

The speedboat, having overtaken them at a furious pace, was now disappearing around the corner that led into the bay where the musical was to be performed. Chloe, sitting in the fishing boat, gripped the wooden bench that was bolted to the sides as the furrow of the wash caused by the speedboat flung itself against them.

A wave of salty sea spray stung her eyes and for a few seconds she kept them tightly shut. When she opened them she could see that Panormitis, their captain, had the vessel under control. Born and bred on Ceres, Panormitis had been schooled in seafaring since, as a toddler, he'd sat on his father's knee at the helm of this boat.

Chloe relaxed once more, but she could feel her despair deepen. So her worst fears hadn't been unfounded. Seeing them together in an amicable situation today had made her doubts become a real possibility. It looked as if Demetrius and Vanessa really had enjoyed more than a platonic relationship. But, then, why shouldn't they? So long as it had been after she'd gone back to England! Or had it started before she'd gone back? That really would be too awful to contemplate.

She focussed her eyes on the approaching shore, the

beautiful sunlit bay, the preparations already in progress for what was going to be a wonderful day. She mustn't think of her own problems. Her thoughts about Demetrius and Vanessa were pure speculation. She mustn't spoil the day for Rachel and Samantha by brooding.

'Mummy, look at the stage up there on the hillside!' Samantha called out excitedly, shielding her eyes from the sun as she pointed towards the large wooden construction where a carpenter was hammering in the last few nails. 'Rachel, wake up and see the stage!'

'Be quiet, Samantha,' Rachel said tetchily, frowning as she rubbed her eyes. 'Why can't you let me sleep?'

Chloe drew her truculent daughter into the circle of her arms. 'We're here, Rachel. If you're tired, you can stay on the boat and sleep for a bit longer. I'll stay with you and—'

'I don't want to sleep! I want to sing up there on the stage with Samantha.'

Rachel pulled herself away and staggered to her feet. 'There, look, I'm OK now.'

She didn't look OK, but Chloe thought it better to let Rachel test out her own strength. All the children had worked so hard during the weeks of rehearsal for this musical that it would be a pity if she had to drop out at the last minute.

Their boat tied up at the small landing stage. Sara got off first and immediately started to organise all the children who were taking part.

'The dressing area is under the trees there, children,' Sara was calling. 'See the large tent? That's where you'll put your costumes on and...'

Chloe listened to her sister giving out clear instructions to the children she'd been coaching. She was so proud of the way her sister had coped with the extra workload besides her hospital job and the preparations for her wedding at the end of the month. But Chloe knew that anything to do with music wasn't a chore for Sara. It had been a labour of love and the satisfaction Sara got from producing the musical they were all going to hear more than compensated for the effort she'd had to put into it.

'Rachel's not feeling too well, Sara,' Chloe said, as she brought the twins to join the group surrounding her sister.

'Don't worry, I'll keep an eye on her.'

'Thanks, and good luck, Sara! It all looks most impressive. The setting is perfect for a story about Demeter and Persephone. Do you remember when Mum used to read the story to us from that picture-book of Greek mythology we had at home?'

Sara smiled. 'All about Demeter searching for her daughter Persephone who'd been abducted by Hades and forced to live in the darkness of the underworld. That bit used to make me really scared. I remember you used to look under our beds to check that Hades wasn't hiding there.'

Chloe shivered as the childhood memories came rushing back. 'I loved the bit where Persephone escapes into the warm sunlight again and takes care of the plants and flowers and everybody's happy again.'

'That comes over really well in the musical,' Sara broke in enthusiastically. 'All the children sing a lovely song about the magic of spring and…well, you'll hear it soon.'

'I'm looking forward to hearing the whole of the musical rather than just the chorus songs that the girls have been practising. Is there anything I can do to help you, Sara?'

'Would you like to help the children put on their costumes?'

Chloe smiled. 'Of course!' She needed something to stop her from worrying about Demetrius and Vanessa.

Out of the corner of her eye she could see the two of them sitting near the stage, deep in conversation. She felt as if she were in the middle of a nightmare as she watched them.

'Chloe, if you take charge of Rachel and Samantha and these three children here, you could get them dressed up and ready,' Sara said. 'The show starts in about an hour. I say about an hour because we're on GMT.'

Chloe smiled at her sister. 'You mean Greek Maybe Time?'

Sara smiled back. 'You've got it! We'll start when everybody's ready. The performance lasts about an hour and then we'll have the barbecue. After lunch, the soloists from the Ceres musical are going to sing again, followed by a performance by a string quartet who arrived from Rhodes this morning.'

'I must say, it's an ambitious project,' Chloe said. 'Well done, Sara.'

'And well done all the mums and dads who've had to put up with the disruption of all the rehearsals.'

'Come on, children,' Chloe said quickly, as she gathered her group of five children together and made off in the direction of the dressing area.

She didn't want to have time to think about her role as a single mum. She could so easily have involved Demetrius by now in caring for their children. Had she been too stubborn in insisting that he wait until she dared to break the news to her family? And in doing so, had she finally lost him? Or had he never really been hers to lose? Had their affair eight years ago meant nothing to him? Had he simply been toying with her affections?

Helping the excited children into their costumes and putting make-up on their faces was just what Chloe needed to take her mind off the couple sitting up there on the hillside. Her five children were ready well within the appointed time. Chloe put out some little chairs under the trees where it was slightly cooler than in the sweltering tent.

'Try to keep still for a few minutes,' she told them. 'And save your voices for singing.'

She glanced down at Rachel. 'You OK, darling?'

'I'm fine.'

Rachel looked far from fine, but Chloe knew she had to let her daughter do the best she could. She moved away, telling them she would be back in five minutes. She needed to be alone for a short while. Walking under the trees at the side of the shore, she breathed deeply, trying to remain calm. She would get through this day and then—

'Chloe!'

She turned at the sound of Demetrius's voice. He sounded slightly out of breath, as if he'd been hurrying to catch up with her.

'I've only just seen you. I was up there on the hillside, talking to Vanessa.'

'Yes, I saw you, Demetrius.'

Now, why had she said that? It looked as if she'd been spying on them when in reality...in reality she had been spying on them!

'I know what you're thinking, Chloe, but—'

'Do you?'

She drew in her breath. Why did Demetrius have to stand so close to her? Why did he have to wear that enticingly sexy aftershave? That all-pervading scent that followed her around whenever she'd had a luxurious soak in his quaint little bathroom.

'Demetrius, you have no idea what I'm thinking otherwise you wouldn't be flaunting yourself up there with that—'

'Hey, steady on, Chloe!'

Demetrius put out his arms and tried to draw her towards him, but she resisted, sidestepping his advances.

'Chloe, I do believe you're jealous!'

'And why shouldn't I be?'

She was handling this so badly. She sounded like a fishwife! This wasn't how she'd meant to behave. She'd meant to be so calm, so cool, so poised.

She took a deep breath as she tried to salvage her pride. 'Demetrius, because I'm not sure if I can trust you…'

'Chloe, would you like to take your group to the stage, please?'

Sara's voice, calling from the nearby path, interrupted her.

'Chloe, I can explain…'

Again Demetrius was holding out his arms towards her but she turned her back, her eyes blurred with tears as she stumbled her way across the stones at the edge of the shore.

There were seats at the front reserved for the mayor of Ceres and his VIP entourage. The second and third rows were reserved for parents. Having delivered her little group of excited children to their positions at the front of the stage, Chloe chose one of the two remaining seats in the second row.

She could see her mother and father chatting to the mayor in the front row where they'd been given reserved seats. Her father was always classed as a VIP on these occasions. He'd told Chloe this morning that he was looking forward to seeing his granddaughters singing on stage.

For an instant her father, as if sensing her eyes on him, turned round and waved a hand towards her.

Chloe waved back as Pam, sitting next to Anthony, also turned and waved.

The small orchestra began to play the overture. The large audience scattered around the hillside, some on chairs, others on cushions or rugs, settled down to watch and listen as the performance began.

Stavros, the musical director, was standing on a roughly constructed wooden podium. The children had gone quiet as they listened to the music that they knew preceded their first chorus.

'Mind if I join you?'

Chloe started in disbelief at the sound of Demetrius's voice. She swallowed hard as she tried desperately to gather her thoughts. The music was flowing over her. She mustn't think about the disturbing presence beside her but, oh, that aftershave! And he looked so desirable today in sexy jeans that strained over his muscular thighs…those thighs that were pressing against hers as she sat squashed up on this small uncomfortable seat.

She glanced sideways. Demetrius was looking at her with a soulful expression in his eyes. Eyes that held such longing and yet such sorrow.

'Truce?' he whispered hopefully.

'Only if you—'

'Shh!' The man in front of her was frowning around at her in disapproval.

Chloe pursed her lips. It was so frustrating to have Demetrius beside her and not to be able to find out the truth.

If only she could trust him again, she could lean against him now and enjoy the feeling of his body touching hers. She realised she was actually leaning against him. She could feel the hard muscles of his upper arm through the thin cotton of his open-necked shirt. He still had the power to unnerve her even when she was trying—without much success—to remain cool.

The children's choir was moving upstage, preparing to sing the opening chorus. A small ripple of conversation came from the audience as proud parents pointed out their children. Chloe felt as proud as any of them as she watched her beautiful daughters taking their places. Both dressed in scarlet robes, there was no way of telling them apart. Unless you were their mother. Chloe understood every tiny distinctive movement her children made.

'I didn't get this seat by chance,' Demetrius whispered. 'I told the girl selling the programmes I was a parent.'

'Oh, Demetrius, you didn't!'

'I was only telling the truth, Chloe.'

'Yes, but—'

She broke off as the audience fell quiet again. The children had begun to sing. It was a haunting melody, telling of the problems that beset Demeter as she searched for her daughter Persephone. The children were singing beautifully. Chloe could feel tears pricking at the back of her eyes. Demetrius reached across and took hold of her hand.

She'd meant to remain unmoved but at the touch of his fingers she could feel her resolutions melting away. Her treacherous body was taking over again. The haunting sound of the music, the nearness of this man that she'd loved for so long, this man she couldn't stop loving, however hard she tried.

Looking up at their children on the stage, her hand imprisoned in Demetrius's, she felt a wonderful glow of happiness. Whatever happened in the future, she would remember this moment. The first time they'd sat together as parents.

The musical continued with the principal players coming onto the stage, enacting the story, whilst the children in the chorus sang in between the solo scenes.

Chloe was fascinated, entranced by the beauty of the music, but most of all feeling such a sense of relief to be so close to Demetrius. She knew it could possibly be the last time they would sit together like this. At the end of the performance she would have to listen to Demetrius's explanations. She would have to join the real world. She couldn't stay in this fantasy world that she'd created for them as they watched their children on stage.

Demetrius had asked for a truce and this was what she was giving him. So it was her duty to stay calm and enjoy this last few minutes.

The performance eventually drew to a close. All the problems had been sorted out on stage, but not in the real-life scenario that would follow when the final applause had died down. Demetrius was clapping enthusiastically. The children on stage were smiling, bowing to the mayor, some of the little ones waving to their parents. Chloe's eyes were fixed on Rachel and Samantha as she clapped.

Samantha looked radiant, but Rachel's head was lolling to one side, her eyes staring fixedly in front of her. Suddenly, Rachel's legs appeared to buckle beneath her and the audience gasped as she slumped to the floor.

Demetrius was on his feet immediately, moving quickly, getting up onto the stage to gather Rachel into his arms. Chloe followed him and put her arm around Samantha, who was looking devastated by the collapse of her sister.

'Come with me, Samantha,' Chloe said calmly, holding her hand as they walked behind Demetrius and Rachel.

Rachel had opened her eyes as Demetrius had picked her up and carried her off the stage.

'Demetrius, I feel awful,' Rachel said in a faint voice. 'My head aches and my neck's gone all stiff.'

'I'll take care of you, Rachel,' Demetrius said calmly. 'Just rest in my arms and don't talk for the moment.'

'Where's my mum?'

'I'm here, Rachel.' Chloe, holding tightly to Samantha's hand, moved to Demetrius's side.

'She's very hot, Demetrius,' Chloe whispered, trying not to alarm Samantha.

Demetrius carried Rachel into the dressing tent. Chloe hastily covered a wooden bench with a couple of sheets and Demetrius laid Rachel on it. After assuring Samantha that Rachel was going to be OK, Chloe found her a little chair, a picture book and a glass of water.

'Sit here near the door, Samantha, while we look after Rachel,' Chloe said. 'Are you feeling OK?'

Samantha nodded. 'You'll make Rachel better, won't you, Mum?'

Chloe hugged her daughter. 'Of course, darling.'

Leaning over Rachel, Demetrius put his hand on her forehead.

'Tell me exactly how you feel, Rachel.'

'My head aches, my neck's all stiff, I feel hot…no, I don't, I feel cold now… Oh, Demetrius, can I go home? I'm so tired…'

Chloe had been checking Rachel's pulse rate. Much too high. She glanced at Demetrius.

'We ought to go back.'

Demetrius nodded. 'We'll take her into hospital and give her some tests,' he said quietly. 'I don't like the rigidity of the neck and—'

'How's Rachel? How's my little granddaughter?' Anthony came hurrying anxiously into the tent.

Demetrius drew him to one side. 'Chloe and I will go back to Ceres and check her out in the hospital. She has pyrexia, high pulse rate, unexplained headache and rigidity of the neck.'

'You need to get back quickly,' the retired surgeon said tersely. 'Any purpuric spots on her body?'

Demetrius shook his head. 'Not yet. I'm hoping there won't be.'

'I'll leave Rachel in your hands, Demetrius,' Anthony said. 'We're both obviously thinking along the same lines in terms of a diagnosis. I hope to God we're proved wrong.'

'Grandpa!' Rachel held out her hand towards Anthony. 'Did you like the show?'

Anthony clutched his little granddaughter's hand as he smiled down at her. 'It was wonderful, darling. Now, you just keep still and quiet and do everything that Demetrius and Mummy tell you to do, won't you?'

But Rachel had again lost interest in what was going on around her as she closed her eyes and put her head back on the makeshift pillow. Samantha had got up from her little chair and followed her grandfather to look at Rachel.

Anthony put an arm round Samantha's shoulders. 'Rachel isn't feeling well, darling, so Mummy and Demetrius are taking her to the hospital to find out what's the matter. Would you like to stay here for the barbecue and then come back home with Grandma and me?'

'Yes, but can I go to the hospital to see Rachel later, Grandpa?'

'Of course you can. I'll take you there.'

Anthony lowered his voice. 'You'll keep me informed, won't you, Demetrius? If there's any deterioration, I'll come along to the hospital at once.'

'Of course,' Demetrius said.

'I have every faith in you, Demetrius,' Anthony said,

patting Demetrius's shoulder before moving away, holding tightly to Samantha's hand.

'You're going to need a fast boat, Demetrius,' someone said.

Chloe looked up as Vanessa spoke. She hadn't noticed her erstwhile friend standing at the door of the tent. She was moving towards them, her hands outstretched towards Chloe.

For a moment, Chloe held back, but then anxiety about Rachel made her listen to what Vanessa was saying. In a crisis like this you needed all the help you could get. Aversions and opinions were to be set aside.

'I've got the family speedboat moored in the bay. Giorgio can take us back to Ceres town quicker than anybody else.'

'Thanks, Vanessa,' Demetrius said quickly. 'Let's go!'

As the boat sped across the water, Chloe and Demetrius sat in the cabin beside Rachel who had now lapsed into a fretful sleep. Chloe was relieved that Vanessa had remained up on deck. She would have preferred Vanessa to have stayed on at the festival, but as it was Vanessa's boat, Chloe could hardly have suggested that!

It was ironic that Giorgio, the man who'd brought Vanessa over the water to deliver Demetrius's letter eight years ago, should now be the man who was saving the day by taking their daughter to hospital. When Chloe had seen Giorgio at the helm of the speedboat that morning, she hadn't remembered who he was. This was a different speedboat. A newer, more impressive model.

Chloe glanced across the sleeping child to look at Demetrius. He was looking as anxious as she felt.

'Are you thinking what I'm thinking?' she asked quietly.

'You mean, the possibility of meningitis?'

Chloe nodded. 'We can't rule it out until we've done the appropriate tests, can we?'

'I'll do a lumbar puncture as soon as we get Rachel into hospital.'

'My side ward was empty when I came off duty, Demetrius. Provided we haven't had an emergency admission, I'll be able to put Rachel in there. I'll check with Michaelis when I get to the hospital but I'm sure he won't object.'

'Excellent idea. We can both stay with her.' Demetrius reached across and took hold of Chloe's hand. 'She needs us both, Chloe. Whatever has happened between us—'

'Anything I can do?'

Chloe bridled at the sound of Vanessa's voice. She was grateful for the use of this powerful boat but her hostility towards the woman who'd ruined her life was difficult to shake off.

'No, thanks, Vanessa.'

'Some tea, coffee?'

'We're fine,' Demetrius said.

'I would like to explain—' Vanessa began, but Chloe cut her short.

'Vanessa, thank you for lending us your boat. I'm terribly worried about Rachel and I'm not in the mood for explanations.'

'Later perhaps?'

Chloe swallowed hard. Why couldn't the wretched woman just leave them alone? She leaned across her daughter to check her pulse again. It was so fast it was almost impossible to count the rate. She put her hand on Rachel's neck. The rigidity was worsening and Rachel was arching her neck backwards.

Aware that Vanessa had taken the hint and left them alone, Chloe stretched her hand across towards Demetrius. 'It could be meningitis, couldn't it?'

Demetrius took hold of her hand. 'It could. But if it is, we're catching it early enough. There aren't even any red or brown pinprick marks that might turn into purple blotches or blood blisters. We've got all the necessary medication in hospital. We can deal with each stage as it comes along, so we mustn't worry, Chloe.'

Chloe took comfort from the feel of Demetrius's hand enclosing her own. 'It's so difficult not to worry when it's your own child. It's bad enough when it's a patient and you're supposed to be a professional, but when…'

Demetrius stood up and drew Chloe to her feet. Gently he held her against him, stroking her hair until her sobs had died down. Pulling a large white handkerchief from his pocket, he dabbed at her eyes. She looked up at the concerned expression on his face.

'I'm sorry. I didn't mean to…'

Demetrius tightened his embrace. 'It's impossible to stay detached when the patient is your own flesh and blood,' he said gently. 'Cry all you like. Let it all come out.'

'Oh, Demetrius, you're so…' Chloe broke off, remembering that this was supposed to be merely a truce. 'You're so kind,' she finished off.

'Rachel is my child, too,' he said quietly.

At the door of the cabin someone gave a discreet cough. Chloe looked across at Vanessa but neither of them commented on what Demetrius had just said. Now there was one more person who knew the truth about Rachel's paternity. But it was no time to worry about that.

'I came to tell you we're almost in the harbour,

Demetrius,' Vanessa said evenly. 'I've radioed ahead to ask for an ambulance to meet us.'

'Thanks, Vanessa,' Demetrius said.

Rachel opened her eyes and quickly closed them again. 'Can somebody close the curtains? It's so bright in here.'

'Keep your eyes closed, darling,' Chloe said gently. 'We're going to move you from here and it will be bright outside till we get in the ambulance.'

'Photophobia,' Chloe muttered under her breath. An aversion to light was yet another symptom of meningitis.

'We'll soon have Rachel in hospital,' Demetrius said reassuringly.

As soon as Chloe had settled Rachel in her side ward, she assembled the apparatus that Demetrius would need to do a lumbar puncture. She was working on autopilot as she set out the top tier of her trolley—two lumbar-puncture needles, a glass manometer for registering the pressure of the cerebrospinal fluid, three sterile test tubes and a pathological examination form for the laboratory.

'What are you doing, Mum?' Rachel tried to raise her head from the pillow. 'Oh, you've changed into your uniform now. Am I a patient in your hospital?'

The young girl was utterly bewildered as she looked around her at the unfamiliar surroundings. Having slept for the past half-hour, she was completely confused by what was happening to her.

'It's OK, Rachel,' Demetrius said, coming into the side ward and taking hold of his daughter's hand. 'Your mother is going to help me when I check out what's going on inside you. I'm going to take some fluid from your back and test it to see why you're feeling poorly.'

'I think Rachel's gone back to sleep again,' Chloe said,

hoping against hope that their child wasn't lapsing into a coma. 'I'll explain to her later.'

Gently, Chloe moved her daughter onto her left side with her knees so flexed that they were close to her chin. Rachel's spine was arched now, making the spaces between the vertebrae at their widest.

Chloe glanced up at Demetrius as she handed him the local anaesthetic. 'Ready? Is Rachel's position OK for you, Doctor?'

It was an attempt to lighten a tense situation. This was their daughter who was in danger and it was very hard to be professional and objective.

'I'm ready, Sister,' Demetrius said as he began the lumbar-puncture procedure, trying desperately to be simply a good professional doctor who was dealing with a patient.

Chloe watched as Demetrius anaesthetised the area around the vertebrae where the investigation would take place. When Demetrius was satisfied that the area was numb, Chloe handed him a sterile trocar and cannula. Carefully, Demetrius withdrew some cerebrospinal fluid and placed it in the appropriate test tubes.

Chloe labelled the sterile test tubes, instructing a nurse to take them to the pathology lab for immediate inspection.

As the nurse hurried away, Demetrius pulled off his sterile gloves and leaned against Rachel's bed.

'Chloe, phone the path lab and say they must drop everything they're doing and deal with the specimens we've sent them. We want those results back as soon as possible.'

'I've written "Urgent" on the labels, Demetrius.'

'Chloe, phone them as well. For the sake of my peace of mind. And tell them to work on Rachel's other tests that I did as soon as we arrived. We need a report on the blood test and—'

'Demetrius, calm down,' Chloe said gently. 'It's all under control.'

She was surprised at how calm she suddenly felt. Having to cope with a worried father was making her stronger. She was also surprised that she was more worried about Demetrius than herself. He loved Rachel so much. He hardly knew her but the father-daughter bond was already in place.

She sat down on the chair at Rachel's bedside. 'There's nothing more we can do for the moment, Demetrius. We've given Rachel a massive dose of antibiotics. That should start to work on a great number of infective organisms until we can find out the specific cause of Rachel's symptoms. So all we can do is wait…'

'And hope,' Demetrius said, his voice cracking under the strain of trying to stay calm.

They both looked up as Kate came in.

'May I suggest you two take a break,' she said gently. 'The paediatric nurse that Michaelis has requested is on her way from the children's ward and she'll stay in here to special Rachel. Go and have a coffee in the office, Chloe. We'll call you if Rachel wakes up and asks for you.'

Chloe forced herself to smile. 'Thanks, Kate I think we'll take you up on that. Come on, Demetrius. You need a break, too.'

Demetrius, who was looking down at their sleeping daughter, dragged himself away.

'OK, if you say so.' He looked across at Kate. 'But you will call us if there's any change in Rachel's condition, won't you, Kate?'

'Of course.'

Chloe looked out of the window of her office. The sky was diffused with the orange and red glow of sunset. It had been a long day, a very long day, in which she'd experienced every kind of emotion. She was feeling drained of all emotion now as she handed Demetrius another cup of coffee.

'I'll phone the path lab,' Demetrius said, putting the coffee-cup on Chloe's desk.

'Demetrius, they're not going to be able to get on with their work if we keep phoning them,' Chloe said gently. 'They'll let us have all the results as soon as they're ready.'

'I'll go and check on Rachel.'

'You checked five minutes ago. Rachel was still asleep. That paediatric nurse is excellent and will let us know if—'

Someone was knocking on the door.

Chloe called, 'Come in.'

She stiffened as Vanessa walked slowly into the office.

'I told your staff nurse I was a family friend,' Vanessa said, standing awkwardly between the desk and the door.

Chloe drew in her breath at the audacity of the woman. 'What's another lie to a person like you, Vanessa? I'm grateful for the lift back from the festival, but you shouldn't have come here.'

'I want to explain.' Vanessa sat down on a high-backed chair in front of Chloe's desk. Chloe pulled her own chair closer to her usual place at the other side of the desk. She felt more in command of the situation now as she fixed her eyes on Vanessa.

'Go on, I'm listening.'

CHAPTER NINE

THE atmosphere in Chloe's small office was tense. Demetrius was looking decidedly worried about the impending confrontation between Chloe and Vanessa.

'Vanessa, it wasn't a good idea for you to come to the hospital. When I asked you to go with me to the festival today—'

'So you really did ask Vanessa to go with you,' Chloe broke in, as her spirits dropped to an all-time low.

She and Demetrius had been so close over the hours they'd struggled to come to terms with the fact that their daughter might be gravely ill, that the worst might happen and they might lose her. She'd felt such a strong bond with Demetrius again, but now...

'Chloe, I asked Vanessa to go to the festival so that she could meet up with you and explain what happened eight years ago,' Demetrius said evenly. 'I knew you wouldn't want to meet her but I thought that you would have no choice but to listen today.'

'Go on, I'm listening, Vanessa,' Chloe said, in a dreary voice.

Vanessa leaned forward and looked across the desk at Chloe with pleading eyes. 'First of all I want to say how sorry I am that I messed up your life, Chloe. I valued your friendship that summer.'

'And I valued yours, Vanessa,' Chloe said quietly. 'But come to the point. Who wrote the letter? Were you and Demetrius...?'

'I wrote the letter,' Vanessa said. 'And, no, there was

nothing between Demetrius and me. But I have to admit I thought that with you out of the way, Demetrius might turn to me and—'

'No chance!' Demetrius broke in heatedly. 'It was a despicable thing to do, Vanessa. Chloe and I were deeply in love. We had a future together.'

'I didn't realise your love was so…so strong,' Vanessa said quietly. 'I knew that Chloe had a boyfriend in England and…'

'Chloe's boyfriend knew that she'd come out to Ceres specifically to decide if there was any future for them,' Demetrius said. 'Chloe had decided to finish their relationship even before she met me. It was only towards the end of her stay here that she started to waver because of the enormity of the step she was taking. That was why Chloe was suffering such emotional turmoil. She had to make a final decision. She confided in you and you betrayed her!'

Demetrius was standing up now, moving across the office to look down at Vanessa with menacing eyes. Chloe hurried from the desk to stand beside him. He reached for her, putting his arm around her shoulder.

Vanessa pushed back her chair and stood up. 'I can only say that I'm terribly sorry for what I did. I didn't realise how much you loved each other. And I had no idea that Chloe was pregnant. How is Rachel?'

For a moment the three were united in the anxiety surrounding Rachel's mysterious illness.

'Her temperature has fallen. The antibiotics must have kicked in,' Chloe said. 'She's sleeping peacefully at the moment. A paediatric nurse is with her and we're waiting for the test results. Vanessa…'

Chloe held out her hand. 'It was a long time ago. I'm going to try to forgive you. I can never forget that you changed the course of my life, but in time I expect I'll be able to forgive.'

Vanessa clutched at Chloe's hand. 'Oh, Chloe, I do hope so. We were such good friends that summer.'

Vanessa looked up at Demetrius. 'Take care of Chloe. Make her happy again.'

Demetrius gave a sad smile. 'If she'll let me.' He held out his hand. 'Goodbye, Vanessa.'

'Goodbye, Demetrius.' Vanessa turned to look at Chloe. 'It really is goodbye. We've sold the house at long last. I'm flying home tomorrow. I've got a boyfriend waiting for me to give him an answer.'

She pulled a wry expression as she stood in the doorway. 'Seeing you two just now, so much in love but not daring to admit it, I've decided. I'm going home to get married.'

Vanessa had gone. There was just the two of them left in the office. Demetrius drew Chloe against him.

'Vanessa did wreak havoc with our lives, but she's right about one thing. We are very much in love…at least I'm in love with you, Chloe, and if you're feeling half as much of what I feel…'

'Yes, Demetrius, I do love you but—'

Demetrius lowered his head and kissed her gently on the lips. He'd heard too many buts. He wanted to savour Chloe's words. She loved him! That was enough for the moment. That was a step in the right direction because for the last few days he'd felt she didn't like him at all. The last week had been almost as bad as the time she'd gone back to England.

He could feel her body responding as she clung to him, her lips meshing with his.

There was a knock on the door. Chloe pulled herself away and called, 'Come in.'

Her father, clutching Samantha's hand, stepped into the office.

'Samantha!' Chloe moved quickly to hug her daughter and lift her onto her lap. 'Are you OK, my love?'

Samantha nodded, leaning her head against her mother's shoulder. 'I wanted to see Rachel before I went to bed so Grandpa said he'd bring me to the hospital.'

'How's Mum?' Chloe asked her father.

'She's worried, but she thought it might be too much for Rachel if we all came to visit. Thanks for your phone calls. Pam sat by the phone from the minute we got back home. So Rachel is still holding her own?'

The paediatric nurse came into the office before Chloe could answer.

'Is there any change in Rachel's condition?' Chloe said.

'She's asking for you, Sister. And her temperature has dropped dramatically. I would say there's a marked improvement in Rachel's condition. But perhaps you and Demetrius would like to come and see for yourself.'

'We certainly would,' Demetrius said.

The phone rang. Chloe picked it up. She was smiling as she listened for about half a minute before putting the phone down again.

'That was the path lab. Rachel hasn't got meningitis. It's some kind of septicaemia which should respond to the antibiotics we've already given her. They're sending up a report as soon as they've got it printed out.'

The paediatric nurse was smiling. 'That's great news. I'll go back to Rachel.'

Demetrius turned to look at Chloe. 'It was obviously one of those childhood illnesses that come on quickly and scare the living daylights out of the parents. I think I'll be a much more sympathetic doctor after today's harrowing experience.'

Samantha climbed off Chloe's lap and took hold of her hand. 'Can we go to see Rachel now?'

The paediatric nurse was waiting outside the door of the side ward when Chloe, Demetrius, Anthony and Samantha arrived.

'Rachel is out of danger now,' she told Chloe. 'Dr Michaelis has arranged for another nurse to help me take care of your daughter during the night so there's no need for you to stay on. I expect you need your sleep.'

'You're very thoughtful,' Chloe said.

She was thankful that the option of a good night's sleep was available but she would come to a decision when she'd seen Rachel.

Rachel was propped up against her pillows. In spite of having slept for the last few hours, she still looked tired. The fever had taken away her strength. It would be a few days before she would be able to move around much again.

Chloe embraced her daughter, hugging her close. 'You're going to be all right, Rachel. How do you feel now?'

Rachel rubbed her eyes. 'Sleepy. Is the festival over?'

'I'm afraid it is,' Demetrius said, moving closer to the bed.

'That's a pity. I didn't want to miss the barbecue.' She looked across at her sister. 'Hi, Samantha, did you save me one of those sausages we saw when we first arrived?'

'I didn't think you'd want any food if you were poorly.'

'We'll arrange a barbecue with lots of sausages when you come out of hospital,' Anthony said. 'You'll probably have to stay in hospital for a few more days but—'

'Will you be here to look after me, Demetrius?' Rachel asked, reaching out to take hold of his hand.

'I'll be with you as much as I can, Rachel,' Demetrius said, sitting down on the edge of the bed. 'I'll have to do some work here in the hospital tomorrow but—'

'Mum told me how hard you worked. She said that was why you couldn't come over to see us as often as you would like to. I know you're a good doctor because I remember how kind you were when I felt horrible today.'

Rachel raised her head from the pillow and held out her little arms towards Demetrius.

'Thank you for being so kind to me, Demetrius. I felt very safe when you were taking that stuff from my back. I wasn't really asleep. I just kept on dozing off and then you made my back go all cold. It wasn't too painful when you put that syringe thing in my back, but I knew you were making me better.'

The little girl put her arms around Demetrius's neck. 'I know you're only a doctor doing your work, but I'd love to have a daddy like you. I sometimes wish you really were my daddy. Most of my friends have daddies but I haven't had a daddy since I was a baby.'

Chloe blinked back the tears as she listened to her daughter's soft, endearing, childish voice. Rachel was still clinging to Demetrius and Chloe could see his shoulders were shaking.

Anthony had moved away from the bedside to allow Chloe, Demetrius and Samantha more space nearer to Rachel.

'I'm just going to slip away for a while. Too many people round the bed. I'll wait outside for you.' Anthony reached forward and kissed Rachel on the cheek. 'Goodnight, my precious.'

Rachel's little arms clung round her grandpa's neck for a few moments before she released him.

'Goodnight, Grandpa. I love you.'

'I love you, too.' Anthony said gently.

The door closed behind him. Chloe sat down on the chair at the other side of the bed to Demetrius, pulling Samantha onto her lap. 'Would you both like to have Demetrius as your daddy?' Chloe asked gently.

Rachel's eyes widened in amazement.

Samantha turned her head to look up at her mother. 'You mean he really could be?'

Rachel was looking puzzled now. 'But I thought you had to plant seeds in tummies and all of that stuff you told me about.'

Chloe looked at Demetrius for some help.

'Sometimes the process can be a bit more complicated than usual,' he said gently. 'Sometimes the mummy might not know the seed in her tummy is growing into a baby and she might go away from the daddy.'

'That would be a pity,' Rachel said.

'I think mummies and daddies should stay together,' Samantha said.

'So do I,' Chloe said. 'But if you'd really like Demetrius to be your daddy...I think it could be arranged.'

Rachel leaned forward, her eyes shining with excitement. 'Wow! That's fantastic!'

'Can we call you Daddy?' Samantha asked.

For once Demetrius looked lost for words. 'I'd like that very much, but for the moment...'

'Of course you can call Demetrius Daddy,' Chloe said quickly as she looked across the bed at him. 'Our own little family unit is the most important aspect of our lives, so let's make the most of it. Life's too short to waste our precious time together.'

'Mum, what are you talking about?' Samantha asked.

Rachel was leaning back on the pillows again, her eyes glazing over. 'Don't keep on asking questions, Samantha. Mum and Demetrius—I mean Daddy—know what they're talking about. It's too complicated to think about now. I'm going to sleep again.'

Demetrius leaned forward and kissed Rachel's cheek. 'All this talking is making you tired. We'll answer questions when you're really better. We're all going to go away now and get some sleep. There'll be a nurse in here with you all night and we'll see you again in the morning.'

Tiptoeing out of the door, hand in hand with Demetrius and Samantha, Chloe heard Rachel whisper, 'Goodnight, Mum, goodnight, Daddy.'

The paediatric nurse sitting outside the door got up from her chair.

'Rachel is sleeping again,' Chloe said. 'We're going home to get a few hours' sleep but you can phone me on my mobile during the night if there's any change. The number's on this card…'

Anthony was waiting for them at the end of the corridor. He drew Chloe to one side.

'Let me take Samantha home by myself. I think you and Demetrius need some time to yourselves.'

'Dad, are you sure you…?'

Anthony squeezed his daughter's hand. 'Of course I'm sure.'

He looked down at Samantha. 'Come on, let's go home to Grandma. Mummy is going to stay with Demetrius tonight. They've got lots to talk about.'

'Not Demetrius. We call him Daddy now.'

'That's nice.' Anthony smiled across at Demetrius. 'I'm glad we're getting things sorted.' He bent down and touched Samantha's shoulder. 'Would you like to keep a secret?'

Samantha looked up at her grandfather. 'What secret?'

'I'd like you to keep it secret from Grandma and Maria and Manolis that Demetrius is going to be your daddy. Just until tomorrow when all the grown-ups are going to have a discussion about it. Do you think you can do that?'

'Of course I can.'

'Come to breakfast, Demetrius,' Anthony said. 'I'll arrange with Michaelis that your work at the hospital is covered for the first part of the morning. OK?'

'Fine!'

Demetrius and Chloe saw Anthony and Samantha out of the hospital and into Anthony's car. As they drove away, Chloe said,

'We haven't told the girls the whole truth yet.'

'We will,' Demetrius said. 'I've promised to answer all their questions. That's the best way of dealing with it. As and when they want to know more, we'll explain in small doses. Children can only take so much at a time. As they get older, maybe they'll begin to understand the dilemma we were in.'

'The dilemma we've still got to dig ourselves out of,' Chloe said. 'We still haven't told my mother or Sara. Francesca arrives soon for the wedding. She'll need to know. And with Sara's wedding in the offing, Mum's already panicking about all the arrangements and the guest list.'

'Stop worrying, Chloe. We can't make any more revelations until tomorrow. Tonight belongs to us,' Demetrius said, his voice husky with emotion.

Lying back in Demetrius's bed, Chloe couldn't remember when she had ever felt so happy. Her body still tingled with the lingering sensations of their love-making.

Demetrius, propped up on his arm beside her, touched her cheek gently.

'You're not still worrying, are you? Wondering how your mother is going to take it?'

'A bit, but we'll see. Now that our daughter is safe, now that our relationship is all coming out in the open, and...'

'And now that we're going to be married...' Demetrius said, a rakish smile on his lips.

'Had we got that far?'

'Just testing! I asked you once before if you would marry me. If I ask you again, will the answer be more favourable?'

Chloe could feel happiness oozing from every passionately satiated pore of her body. She snuggled closer. 'It might be. Try me.'

'Shall I get out of bed and go down on one knee?'

She put her arms around his neck. 'Please, don't! Stay here. I'm feeling very...well, ask the question first...'

'Chloe, will you marry me, darling?'

'Yes, oh, yes,' she breathed as she moulded herself against him, feeling the hard, exciting response of his muscular body...

The shrilling of a mobile awakened her. Demetrius was reaching out towards the bedside table.

'It's mine,' Chloe said. 'I hope it's not the hospital... Oh, hi, Dad! Yes, we're just going to get ready. We have to see Rachel first and then we'll be with you.'

Chloe rang off.

Demetrius drew her into the circle of his arms. 'Everything OK?'

'Yes, Dad's organised a family breakfast. He wants us all to be together when we make our announcement. He's squared it with Michaelis in his capacity of hospital medical director. In fact, Michaelis is going to be there, and Sara. Well, it's less than three weeks to their wedding so Michaelis will soon be part of the family. He's entitled to take an interest.'

'He's a clever man, your father,' Demetrius said. 'I'm glad we've got him on our side at last.'

'I don't think it's a question of taking sides,' Chloe said reflectively. 'Knowing Dad, he'll want to be very fair. But Mum can be very highly strung and she tends to worry herself silly about small details.'

'Chloe, this is hardly a small detail—you and I announcing we're going to be married, explaining how it came about that I'm the twins' father and—'

Chloe groaned. 'Don't remind me. That's why I couldn't face it before…before I realised that life without you wouldn't be worth living. When we were waiting to get the results of Rachel's tests yesterday I knew that whatever happened, you and I had to be together. I was even ready to fight Vanessa for you if I had to!'

Demetrius smiled. 'I'm glad you didn't need to do that.' He picked up his mobile. 'I'll phone the hospital to get a report on Rachel and tell them we'll be in to see her soon. After that we'll go over to your house and face the family.'

Rachel was sitting up in bed, nibbling on a piece of toast, when they arrived at the hospital. She greeted them enthusiastically.

'I feel so much better. Don't you think I could come home, Demetrius…I mean, Daddy? You could do the barbecue, couldn't you?'

'You're making such good progress that I'll try to get you out in a couple of days, but today would be too soon,' Demetrius said gently.

'OK. Would you like some of my toast?'

'No, thanks. Your mum and I have to go over to see your grandparents for breakfast, let them know how you're getting on.'

'But you will come back, won't you, Dad? Seems funny, calling you that, but I do like it.'

'Of course I will.'

As Demetrius helped her down from the car, Chloe looked up at the house and felt a shiver of apprehension. This wasn't going to be easy. The end of the lie she'd been living for eight years. The shattering of a dream for her mother. The recriminations, the accusations.

But it was something they had to do. They had to put the record straight before she and Demetrius and their daughters could begin their life together as a family.

'I thought we'd have breakfast on the terrace,' Pam said as soon as Chloe and Demetrius had climbed up to the house.

'Mum, where's Samantha? She usually comes rushing out to meet me.'

'Samantha's had breakfast and she's helping Manolis in the back garden. She doesn't know you're here so I should leave her where she is for a while. Now, come along and join the others. This was Anthony's idea. He's being very mysterious. I think it's a thanksgiving celebration that poor little Rachel isn't in the throes of meningitis. So worrying for all of us, wasn't it?'

Chloe could tell her mother was nervous by the incessant flow of chatter that she kept up as they went through the house and out onto the terrace. It was a perfect morning for an outdoor breakfast. She looked across the water to the hills beyond, trying to draw strength and courage from the beauty that surrounded her. There wasn't a ripple of wind to ruffle the mirror-like surface of the bay and the hot August sun was already warming the stones on the terrace.

'Good morning, Dad. What a lovely day!'

Start as you mean to go on, Chloe thought as she breezed up to plant a kiss on her father's cheek.

'Are you OK?' he whispered.

'I'm fine!' Chloe said, still smiling as she sat down beside her father.

Her mother, on Anthony's other side, was busy with the coffee-pot. Demetrius sat down next to Chloe and squeezed her hand under the table.

Sara, sitting with Michaelis on the other side of Demetrius, leaned across to whisper to Chloe, 'What's the big secret?'

Chloe picked up her coffee-cup and took a large gulp. 'I think we'd better get on with—'

'Chloe, before you say anything,' Anthony intervened, placing a hand over his daughter's, 'I would prefer to put everybody in the picture. I'd like to explain what's happening.'

He looked around the table at everybody. Even his wife had now fallen silent. 'Eight years ago, Demetrius came to me and asked for Chloe's hand in marriage.'

Pam gave a gasp of surprise.

'Yes, my dear. I didn't tell you at the time because you were planning an engagement party and I knew you wouldn't want to be worried by this latest twist of events. Demetrius and Chloe were very much in love and so, of course, Chloe knew she had to make a choice. Rightly or wrongly, she chose to go back to England and become engaged to Patrick.'

'So now they've got together again,' Pam said quietly. She looked across the table at Chloe. 'I could see you were fond of each other but I hadn't realised that you'd been in love before.'

'Yes, we were very much in love,' Demetrius said, putting his arm around Chloe in a protective gesture as her bravado began to evaporate.

He could feel her trembling against him and knew she was dreading having to reveal that he was the father of the twins.

'One result of our love affair is now a joy to us both,' Demetrius continued quietly. 'We've decided that it's time we told you the whole truth. I am the proud father of our beautiful twins.'

Pam sat in stunned silence, staring at Chloe.

Sara turned to Demetrius. 'I must admit, there were times when I wondered if the girls really were Patrick's. And there were times after Patrick died when I hoped that my vague theory might be correct.' A slow smile spread across her face. 'Welcome to the family, Demetrius.'

'I never doubted it,' Anthony said quietly. 'But I went along with whatever Chloe wanted me to think.'

He turned to Demetrius and held out his hand. 'Welcome to the family, Demetrius.'

The two men shook hands.

Demetrius cleared his throat. 'When I came to ask for Chloe's hand in marriage before, you said that if Chloe agreed she wanted to marry me, you would give us your blessing. I'm happy to say that I was luckier this time than eight years ago. Earlier this morning, Chloe agreed to marry me.'

'Well, I hope you're not planning to have a wedding too soon after Sara's,' Pam said, her ashen face showing that she was still in a state of shock. 'I've only just got this one organised and I really couldn't take—'

'Why don't we have a double wedding?' Sara burst in enthusiastically. 'The same church, the same reception, the same guests—apart from the ones that Demetrius and Chloe will want to add to the list…'

'Sara, steady on…' Anthony said. 'I think that's a brilliant idea, but what do Chloe and Demetrius think?'

'I think it would be fantastic,' Demetrius said. 'The sooner we're married, the better.'

Chloe turned to her sister. 'Won't you mind sharing your big day?'

'I'll love it!' Sara said, turning to look at Michaelis. 'Would you be happy to share our day, Michaelis?'

Michaelis smiled. 'It would be excellent. Take some of the pressure off me if there's another bridegroom around. The only thing I'm interested in is the fact that we'll be married at the end of the long ceremony and be able to get on with our lives again.'

Sara leaned across the table to grasp her mother's hand. 'Mum, stop worrying about the wedding. You've done all the hard work already. Chloe and I will take over now. All we'll need is a special licence for Chloe and Demetrius. We'll have to talk to the priest and—'

'And I'll need a wedding dress,' Chloe said, still shell-shocked by the rapidity of the unfolding events.

Yesterday morning her relationship with Demetrius had been at an all-time low. Today it already felt as if he was part of her family and they had formed their own little family unit. She turned to look at him. He was pushing back his chair, reaching out to take hold of her hand.

'Thanks for breakfast,' Demetrius said quietly.

'But you've hardly eaten anything,' Pam said.

'I'm not hungry.'

Chloe smiled. 'Neither am I. Did you say Samantha is in the back garden with Manolis, Mum?'

'Yes, your father said to keep her out of the way until we'd had breakfast. She thinks you're still at the hospital.'

'We'll go and find her,' Demetrius said.

'We've got so much to tell her,' Chloe said happily.

She went round the table to where Pam was sitting. Leaning down, she kissed her mother's cheek. 'Don't be sad, Mum.'

Pam turned her head and smiled up at her daughter. 'I'm not sad, darling. So long as you're happy, that's all that matters. It will take me a while to adjust to all the changes in our lives, but I'll get there in the end. I suppose the important thing is to look to the future. We can't change the past, can we?'

'We certainly can't.'

Pam stretched out her hand towards Demetrius. 'Welcome to the family, Demetrius!'

CHAPTER TEN

As THE boat approached Ceres harbour Chloe looked up at the imposing white façade of Ayios Nikolas. Set on the side of the hill, this was the church where she was to be married this morning. She could feel her excitement mounting. She was trying desperately to remain calm because it was going to be a long day and she didn't want to be too exhausted to enjoy her honeymoon night with Demetrius.

There were so many people in the combined wedding parties that Anthony had hired several boats to transport everyone to Ceres harbour. This was where Chloe and Sara would begin the wedding procession to meet their bridegrooms. Demetrius and Michaelis would be walking from the upper town in a procession consisting of their own families and friends.

Sara reached out and touched Chloe's hand. 'Are you feeling as nervous as I am?'

Chloe nodded. 'I know Demetrius and Michaelis have told us what to expect, but a Greek wedding does seem a bit complicated, doesn't it?'

'What are you two whispering about?' Pam came to stand in front of her daughters. 'Not scared, are you?'

Chloe gave a nervous smile. 'Petrified!'

'So am I,' Sara said.

'Well, you both look fabulous! I feel so proud of my daughters.' Pam leaned forward to kiss them both on the cheek. 'I'm so glad you both spent the whole of last week at home. I couldn't have managed without you.'

'I enjoyed it,' Chloe said. She reached out to squeeze her mother's hand. 'I really feel as if I've got to know you again, Mum.'

Chloe lowered her voice. 'I didn't like having to pretend that Patrick was the twins' father. It was what Patrick wanted. I just thought it would be less hurtful to everybody. But now it's all out in the open and you've all accepted it, I feel so happy.'

Pam leaned forward and hugged her daughter. 'Chloe, I've come to realise that you had no choice, and I respect you for considering everybody's feelings. I know you're going to be happy. Demetrius is a wonderful man. And the twins adore him.'

Pam turned to look at Sara. 'I'm glad we went along with your idea of a double wedding. I can tell it's going to be a great day. We're almost there. Gather up your skirts, girls.'

As their mother moved out of the cabin, Chloe turned to her sister. 'Mum looks radiant, doesn't she? I love that cream silk suit she's wearing. All that worrying she did and now she's in control of everything.'

'I think she really appreciated having us at home,' Sara said. 'And we all drew much closer as a family, didn't we?'

'Pity that Francesca only arrived last night,' Chloe said. 'We haven't had time to get to know her again. Where is she, by the way?'

'She said she'd follow later. I don't think Francesca wanted to join in the procession.'

'I'm not too happy about it myself,' Chloe said. 'Francesca was very quiet at supper last night, wasn't she? Considering we haven't seen her for ages, she didn't tell us very much about what's been happening to her, did she?'

'I think she's had a tough time. Working as a doctor in a busy London hospital is pretty exhausting. And then there was that disastrous relationship that broke up. She hasn't told us anything about that, has she?'

'She will,' Chloe said. 'Give her time. I hope she'll spend some time out here and not go rushing back. Ever since she got that high-powered job in the London hospital we haven't seen enough of her. She's such good fun, isn't she?'

Sara stood up. 'Remember how she used to try and boss us around because she was the oldest? We used to play tricks on her and then we'd all finish up giggling together and she'd forget she'd been trying to be boss.'

'She hasn't changed, has she? Everybody who's worked with her says she's a brilliant doctor. She was always the strong, competent one. I always used to look up to her and want to be like her. Clever, brainy, beautiful, talented. I think she was tired last night after the journey but she'll have recovered today.'

'I'd love to know why she split up with her boyfriend. They'd been together for ages when, out of the blue, she told us it was all over.'

Sara glanced over the water. 'We're nearly there. Are you ready?'

Chloe smoothed down the silk folds of her wedding dress. 'As ready as I'll ever be.'

As the two sisters alighted from the boat onto the quayside, there was a ripple of spontaneous applause from the waiting crowds of tourists and local people. It seemed as if the whole of Ceres had turned out to greet them.

The first thing that Chloe had done after agreeing to their double wedding had been to call in Sara's dressmaker. A talented lady living on the other side of the island, she had come over to the house, drawn up designs and produced the most exquisite white gown. As Chloe walked forward now over the rough cobbles of the harbour, she felt like a queen. All her nerves had disappeared as she felt the rustle of her silk skirts around her. The tightly fitting bodice with its low-cut neckline was very flattering and the ruched sleeves tapering to her wrists made her feel positively elegant.

And Sara's white gown was equally beautiful. The heavily embroidered satin had tiny gemlike stones stitched to the hemline which sparkled in the bright morning sunlight.

'I feel like somebody else,' Chloe whispered to her sister, who was walking beside her.

'You look like somebody else. So do I. I hope Demetrius and Michaelis will be able to recognise us. They'll be walking down the hill in their procession now… Oh, look, there's Dad arriving in the boat with Rachel and Samantha! Don't your little girls look beautiful in their bridesmaids' dresses? You must be so proud of them.'

The twins hitched up their long skirts above their knees and leapt onto the quayside, hurrying over the cobblestones to walk behind Chloe and Sara. The crowd parted to let them through and an undercurrent of admiring comments became audible as the little girls passed.

The iron bell of Ayios Nikolas was pealing out across the water as the wedding procession made its way to the foot of the hill. Chloe could feel her excitement mounting. This was where the Metcalfe family procession had arranged to meet the procession headed by Demetrius and Michaelis.

The bridegrooms' procession was there already! As the crowd parted, Chloe could see Demetrius, tall and proud, looking so handsome in his dark suit that she felt her knees going weak with the thought that tonight she would lie in his arms, Demetrius's bride, his wife for the rest of their time on this earth, the father of her children...

Her feet were propelling her towards him, but she had no recollection of making any physical movement as she was drawn, as if by magic, towards the Greek god standing at the front of the procession. Michaelis, beside him, looked handsome and debonair, but Chloe only had eyes for Demetrius, her soon-to-be husband.

Demetrius was stepping forward, coming to meet her. She tried to look poised and calm but at the last moment she broke away from her procession and moved swiftly towards Demetrius. She didn't know what tradition decreed at this point but Demetrius saved the day by leaning forward and giving her a chaste kiss.

The onlookers began clapping again.

'You look wonderful!' Demetrius said, before bending down to speak to the twins. 'And so do you.'

Both girls reached up to kiss Demetrius simultaneously on each cheek. There was another ripple of approval from the people watching.

Demetrius turned back to look at his bride, taking her hand and beginning to walk up the wide path that led to the church.

As soon as Demetrius took hold of her hand, all Chloe's nerves disappeared. Demetrius would know the form inside the church. All she had to do was relax and enjoy the day. She would never have another wedding day so she was going to enjoy it. And afterwards...

They were walking into the church. She daren't begin to think about afterwards just yet. She put up a hand to check that her rose-bedecked headband hadn't slipped and then she and Demetrius moved forward to join Michaelis and Sara in the centre of the church.

The first thing that struck her was the informality of the

occasion. Mothers with young babies were chatting happily as they crowded forward to get a better view of the proceedings. Children laughed and played in the aisles between the wooden pews, generating their own air of excitement to add to the general feeling of thanksgiving. It seemed more like Christmas morning, opening presents around a family tree, than a solemn ceremony!

But why should weddings be solemn? she thought, remembering the strained atmosphere at some of the English weddings she'd been to. A wedding was a time of rejoicing. And this was just the sort of atmosphere she needed to make her relax. It didn't detract from the solemnity of the occasion—rather, it enhanced the joyous celebration of committing yourself for ever to someone you loved.

Out of the corner of her eye, she saw Francesca coming into the church. She looked tall and beautiful as always in a well-cut, expensive-looking, light-coloured suit. Francesca smiled and waved towards her sisters. Chloe and Sara waved back.

Chloe leaned across towards Sara and whispered, 'Doesn't Francesca look fabulous today?'

Sara nodded. 'All she needed was a good night's sleep. You OK, Chloe?'

'Never been so happy in my life!'

The priest, in long white robes, was intoning a monologue now, sometimes speaking, sometimes chanting.

'I can't understand what he's saying,' Chloe whispered to Demetrius.

Demetrius smiled. 'So long as you understand that we're getting married, it doesn't really matter.'

'I'm so glad I can talk to you during the ceremony,' Chloe said. 'It's all so beautifully informal.'

'I'm glad you're enjoying it.' Demetrius linked his fingers through hers. 'The best is yet to come.'

'I know.' She looked up into his eyes and felt a shiver of desire running down her spine.

Still continuing with the incantation, the priest moved forward and began putting ribbons around Demetrius and herself, knotting them together to signify that they were now joined in holy matrimony.

A second priest was doing the same to Michaelis and Sara. Chloe wondered if this was the mystical moment when they actually became husband and wife. It felt like it. She really felt at one with Demetrius now. Out of the corner of her eye she could see Rachel and Samantha watching wide-eyed. She smiled at them and they smiled happily back.

'Are you married yet, Mum?' Rachel said.

Chloe smiled. 'Yes, we're married.'

As if in confirmation of this, the bell, which had been silenced at the beginning of the ceremony, started to ring out again.

Demetrius bent his head and kissed her on the lips. This time his kiss was demonstratively tender but not inappropriately so. Chloe knew he was holding himself back, as she was.

Demetrius, now holding her tightly by the hand, was taking her towards the door. The guests were kissing each other, people were coming forward to kiss the brides, to kiss the six little bridesmaids, to congratulate the bridegrooms. Sara and Michaelis came across to join them and there were more kisses.

At last Demetrius and Chloe reached the porch and were able to escape into the bright sunlight. The crowd of well-wishers who hadn't been able to get into the church cheered. The photographers surged forward. They hadn't had a double wedding before so this was the event of the year for them.

Rachel was tugging at her mother's skirts. 'When are we going home, Mum?'

'You mean back to Grandma and Grandpa's?'

Rachel grinned. 'Oh, yes, that's not my home any more, is it? We're going to live in Daddy's house, aren't we? That's going to be great. We'll be able to walk from there to school, won't we, Samantha?'

Samantha smiled happily. 'Natasha lives just around the corner from Daddy's house. She'll be able to come and play, won't she, Mum?'

'Of course she will.'

Chloe gathered up her skirts, preparing for the final walk down the hill back to the boat. The caterers would have set out all the food and drink back at the house in Nimborio. Maria and Manolis had already left the church to hurry back and take charge of the proceedings, but Chloe wanted to get back as soon as she could to make sure everything was going according to plan.

They were alone at last! The reception had gone without a hitch, the guests had all departed. Demetrius had taken Chloe back to his house in the upper town, after they'd put the twins to bed at the house in Nimborio.

Chloe breathed a sigh of relief as she kicked off her shoes and lay back against the sofa cushions in the upstairs sitting room that had the fabulous view towards the sea. She loved this room. It was so cosy, so comfortable… She gave a shiver of happiness. She loved every part of this house, the house where she and Demetrius were going to spend the rest of their lives together.

Demetrius put his arm around her shoulders and drew her against him.

'You don't mind spending your wedding night at home, do you, Chloe?'

'Mind? This is my idea of bliss. It was my choice not to go away, remember? I wanted the first night to be here in your…I mean our house so that it begins to feel like home. Tomorrow we'll bring the girls over. Later in the year, when we've all settled in, we can take a holiday somewhere else if we want to. But as Ceres is the most beautiful place on earth, I'm happy to stay here for the rest of my life.'

'I'm glad you're happy on my island.'

'How could I not be? I've got everything I'd ever wished for.'

'It took a long time to get it together but we've finally made it.' Demetrius was reaching over the back of the sofa for the ice-bucket.

'I thought we'd have a nightcap,' he said, lifting the bottle of champagne from the ice.

Chloe put a restraining hand on his arm. 'Could we carry the whole lot upstairs? If we were in bed, we could really relax.'

Demetrius kissed her provocatively on the lips. 'I don't think relaxing is exactly the right way to describe our honeymoon night, do you?'

Chloe put her arms around his neck. 'I'll tell you tomorrow morning, darling…'

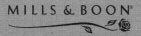

MILLS & BOON®

Medical Romance™

THE SURGEON'S SECOND CHANCE
by Meredith Webber

Harry had loved Steph when they were medical
students – but she married Martin. Now Steph is a
widow – and Harry is back in town…and back in love!
Harry knows he and Steph should be together, and
he's not going to miss his second chance. He has to
prove that she can trust him. But it won't be easy…

SAVING DR COOPER *by Jennifer Taylor*

A&E registrar Dr Heather Cooper isn't looking for
love. But when she crosses paths with a daring
firefighter she's frightened by the strength of her
emotions. Ross Tanner isn't afraid of danger. To him,
life is too short not to live it to the full – and he's
determined to show Heather that his love for her is
too precious to ignore.

EMERGENCY: DECEPTION *by Lucy Clark*

Natasha Forest's first day as A&E registrar at Geelong
General Hospital held more than medical trauma. She
came face to face with the husband she had thought
dead for seven years! A&E director Dr Brenton
Worthington was equally stunned. Somebody had
lied, and Brenton needs to discover the truth!

On sale 6th June 2003

*Available at most branches of WH Smith,
Tesco, Martins, Borders, Eason, Sainsbury's
and all good paperback bookshops.*

0503/03a

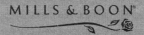

FREE!

2 Books
and a surprise gift!

We would like to take this opportunity to thank you for reading this Mills & Boon® book by offering you the chance to take TWO more specially selected titles from the Medical Romance™ series absolutely FREE! We're also making this offer to introduce you to the benefits of the Reader Service™ —

- ★ FREE home delivery
- ★ FREE gifts and competitions
- ★ FREE monthly Newsletter
- ★ Books available before they're in the shops
- ★ Exclusive Reader Service discount

Accepting these FREE books and gift places you under no obligation to buy; you may cancel at any time, even after receiving your free shipment. Simply complete your details below and return the entire page to the address below. *You don't even need a stamp!*

YES! Please send me 2 free Medical Romance books and a surprise gift. I understand that unless you hear from me, I will receive 4 superb new titles every month for just £2.60 each, postage and packing free. I am under no obligation to purchase any books and may cancel my subscription at any time. The free books and gift will be mine to keep in any case.

M3ZEB

Ms/Mrs/Miss/Mr ....Initials................................
BLOCK CAPITALS PLEASE

Surname ....

Address ....

....

....Postcode ....

Send this whole page to:
UK: The Reader Service, FREEPOST CN81, Croydon, CR9 3WZ
EIRE: The Reader Service, PO Box 4546, Kilcock, County Kildare (stamp required)

Offer not valid to current Reader Service subscribers to this series. We reserve the right to refuse an application and applicants must be aged 18 years or over. Only one application per household. Terms and prices subject to change without notice. Offer expires 29th August 2003. As a result of this application, you may receive offers from Harlequin Mills & Boon and other carefully selected companies. If you would prefer not to share in this opportunity please write to The Data Manager at the address above.

Mills & Boon® is a registered trademark owned by Harlequin Mills & Boon Limited.
Medical Romance™ is being used as a trademark.